Wild Ghost Chase

MONSTERVILLE

Wild Ghost Chase

by R. A. Noonan

ALADDIN PAPERBACKS

Copyright © 1996 by Twelfth House Productions

Aladdin Paperbacks
An imprint of Simon & Schuster
Children's Publishing Division
1230 Avenue of the Americas
New York, NY 10020

First Aladdin Paperbacks edition January 1996

Printed and bound in the United States of America

10 9 8 7 6 5 4 3 2 1

Library of Congress Cataloging-in-Publication Data

Noonan, R. A.
Wild ghost chase / by R. A. Noonan.
p. cm. — (Monsterville ; #4)
Summary: When Brook Lauer encounters a runaway from the Poltergeist Academy in Monsterville, the ghost teaches her to overcome her shyness and speak up for herself.
ISBN 0-689-71866-7
[1. Ghosts—Fiction. 2. Bashfulness—Fiction.] I. Title.
II. Series: Noonan, R. A. Monsterville ; #4.
PZ7.N753Wi 1996
[Fic]—dc20 95-20845

Wild Ghost Chase

Prologue

Help me! I'm a prisoner at the Poltergeist Academy!

It's not as scary as it sounds. But if you could die of boredom, consider me dead.

This place is totally lame. Why did my parents send me here, anyway?

Sure, it's safer than the outside world. The humans don't bother us. And there are more of us here to keep one another company. That's what they said when I first arrived.

Except I never thought humans were that scary in the first place!

Ugh! School! I may as well be mortal, for all the fun I have!

I never get to use my powers.

I never get to haunt anyone.

I never have any fun!

Back at the house where I used to live, I haunted all the time. I scared three different families away!

But do I get any extra credit? No! Do I even get to add my two cents in class? Hardly ever!

I'm just supposed to sit quietly, doing my lessons.

Meanwhile, there's a whole world out there, waiting to be terrified. It's not fair.

Well, I've had enough. I'm busting out of here. Out of the Academy, and out of Monsterville. With all my experience, I don't need a diploma. I already know how to wreak havoc! And I've got a shriek that'll curl your toes!

I've got my powers.

I know how to use them.

It's time to scare the socks off some humans!

The light from the fireplace was flickering eerily in the darkened living room of the Ryan ranch. The mood was absolutely perfect for a good scare! And the story of the phantom cat-lady was always guaranteed to creep everyone out.

"And to this very day, you can still hear the old woman's quavery voice rising through the trees as she roams the forest," Darcy Ryan said in a haunted voice.

Huddled close in their sleeping bags, the other girls didn't dare say a word.

The fire cast shadows over Darcy's long honey blond hair as she spoke. "She's calling, calling out for her beloved cats that she lost forever. *Can you hear her now?*"

"Hey, girls! Want some s'mores?"

"Mom!" Darcy glanced up, peeved. "You ruined my story!"

"Just thought you might want a snack," Pam Ryan said cheerfully. "Don't let me interrupt."

"It's hard to feel spooked when there's a plateful of dessert being handed around," Darcy muttered.

Brook Lauer didn't mind the interruption. That

cat-lady story always gave her the shivers. The idea of the ghostly old lady wandering through the forest . . . Yikes!

"Thanks, Mrs. Ryan," Francie said. With ginger hair and deep green eyes, Francie Capezio was a year older than Darcy. She had moved in with the Ryans just a few weeks ago.

"I love these things," Nora Chambers announced. She helped herself and passed the plate along. Her braces glinted in the firelight as she grinned at Darcy's mom. "Thank you a million times!"

Tucking a strand of carrot red hair behind one ear, Brook watched her friend enviously. Nora was so good at making conversation! She always had something to say.

Nora and Brook were spending the night at Darcy's house. They did stuff like this all the time. The three girls were like the Three Musketeers of Whiterock, Montana.

"We're a perfect team," Nora always said. She was tickled by the fact that Darcy was blond, Brook was a redhead, and Nora herself was brunet. "We're like a hair commercial!"

Tonight they were roughing it and camping out. Well, *sort* of camping out. Actually, they were all cocooned in their sleeping bags in front of the fireplace. Sleeping outside in freezing cold December was too adventurous—even for Darcy.

The plate of marshmallows, chocolate bars, and graham crackers came around to Brook. She drew in her breath so she could thank Mrs. Ryan.

"Thanks for the—," Brook began.

"Mom, you promised to stay upstairs," Darcy cut in. "We can't tell scary stories if you keep coming down here!"

"Okay, okay." Pam Ryan laughed. She put the plate down on the rug near the girls and headed out.

"Thanks, Mrs. Ryan," Brook called out. But Darcy's mom was already gone. She didn't hear Brook—as usual.

It seemed like nobody ever heard what Brook had to say. It was starting to seriously bum her out.

"Okay, my story's ruined," Darcy said, plopping a melted marshmallow onto a cracker. "It's someone else's turn. Brook, you go!"

"Oh!" Brook was surprised. *I thought someone else was going before me. Now, what was that story I was thinking of?* Her mind raced. "Um . . . well . . ." *Shoot!* She had thought of a great idea during Darcy's story. Something about a mysterious hitchhiker. What was it? How was it supposed to start?

"Hey, I've got a great one," Francie announced. "This is really scary. You don't mind, do you, Brook?"

"No, she didn't have one, anyway," Darcy answered for her. "You go ahead."

"Okay." Francie looked at them all with narrowed eyes as she wound up for her story. "Deep in the woods, there lived a hunter with a great hatred of wolves. . . ."

Sheesh! Brook watched Francie start her story, and that envious feeling crept over her again. Francie was new to Whiterock. If Brook had to move to a new town and meet new people, she'd be petrified! But already Francie had made a million friends.

The truth was, Francie was really nice. Kind of small and pixieish, with a pale face and a pointy chin, she was full of energy and spunk. She always had something nice to say. And she was a year ahead of Brook and Darcy in school.

"But wait," Francie said, waving her hands. "This is the best part. . . ."

As Brook listened to the story, her anger began to simmer. Darcy had just assumed she wouldn't care if Francie went ahead of her. How did she know whether Brook wanted to tell a story or not?

Brook stared into the flames of the fire, letting her mind drift. This kind of thing was happening a lot lately. Just yesterday, something terrible happened at school.

At the beginning of the year, their teacher, Ms. Blundell, had asked Brook to carry the attendance sheet to the office each day. Brook loved the job. It was the coolest feeling, being alone in the school hallways while everyone else was in class.

But Ms. Blundell was away on maternity leave. And Ms. Yellowfeather, the substitute, didn't know that Brook was kind of shy.

Anyway, Friday morning, when Ms. Yellowfeather called her, Brook didn't answer right away. Her pencil had fallen under her desk, and she was leaning over to pick it up. Before she could sit up and say that she was ready, Darcy's hand shot up into the air.

6

Brook heard Darcy say, "I'll do it!" and realized what was happening. She opened her mouth to object, but Nora chimed right in.

"I don't think Brook really likes to do the attendance run," Nora had said. "She's kind of shy. Maybe Darcy should do it from now on."

"That would be fine with me," Darcy had said. "You don't mind, do you, Brook?"

Brook had opened her mouth. She meant to say something! But everybody was looking at her. Would she look like a brat if she asked to keep the job? Her mouth went dry. "Uegh—" was all she managed to say.

"No, she doesn't mind," Nora had answered for her.

And Ms. Yellowfeather had just gone along with it—without asking Brook!

But Brook couldn't muster up the courage to say anything. She'd always been the quietest kid in the school. So they just steamrolled over her and expected her to go along with their plans. It really made her want to tell them off! Except . . .

Except she just couldn't. Like right now.

As her mind drifted back to Darcy's living room, Francie was finishing her story.

"The hunter looked behind him. Through the trees, he saw the red eyes of the wolf he had killed. The ghost of the wolf would never let him be!" Francie said in a hushed voice.

Brook checked out her friends' faces, lit by the fire. Rapt and wide-eyed, Darcy and Nora were listening to the creepy story. They didn't know that Brook felt left out.

How do you tell someone you're angry at them? *Excuse me, guys, but when this story's over, I'd really like to tell you about how you hurt my feelings.* That was lame. Maybe she should say: *I have a scary story—about a quiet girl who gets tired of her friends and goes crazy!* Right. They'd think that was a joke!

But it wasn't funny to Brook. It was serious business. Sometimes she felt like she was invisible!

She hunched down in her sleeping bag, feeling miserable.

"So when you hear that howling in the woods, it's really the red-eyed wolf," Francie said. "He's calling . . . calling out to the hunter. Can you hear him?" She let out a howl . . . then giggled.

"Yowww, good story," Nora said, pulling her sleeping bag around her shoulders. "I got a chill."

"Hey, Brook, are you going to sleep?"

Finally! She was getting some attention. They were bound to realize that something was wrong! "Yes," she answered, in a sulky voice. They'd have to ask if something was wrong now!

"Okay, good night," Darcy said cheerily. "Tell us if we're being too loud."

Excuse me? Don't they realize that I'm totally bummed over here?

But the answer was clear. They didn't. Darcy and Nora just went on chatting with Francie. Brook stared at the ceiling, letting tears well up in her eyes.

She felt like the loneliest person in the world.

Sunday morning brought a big blue Montana sky. It had snowed the night before, and the pine trees around the meadow were covered with fluffy whiteness. As Brook drew her breath in through her nose, she felt the delicious crisp coldness of the air. The whole world looked brand new.

But Brook still had the same old problems.

"Guys, check it out. I'm going to jump over all *three* logs this time!" Darcy announced.

Brook sat on a horse, next to Francie and Nora, as they watched Darcy practice her tricks.

Darcy was a skilled rider. After all, her mom owned a ranch, and she'd been riding horses since she was two years old. Her horse, Gingersnap, kicked up little puffs of snow as they trotted around the meadow.

It seems like everybody's good at something, Brook thought sadly. *Except dumb old me.*

Francie and Nora cheered as Darcy and Gingersnap executed a graceful leap over a pile of logs.

"That was stellar," Francie exclaimed.

"Brook, did you see that?" Nora wanted to know.

"Yup," Brook said.

"Darcy's so good at horseback riding," Nora babbled. "I wish I was a better rider. But it's a major effort for me to just stay in the saddle."

"I know," Brook muttered.

"I know you know," Nora gabbed. "The only thing I'm good at is sledding. That's not the same as horseback riding. Know what I mean?"

"Yup."

"Making a horse jump like that is too weird," said Nora. "Is it like flying? Or do you want to throw up like on the teacup ride at the fair? Remember that time I almost threw up on that ride?"

Brook sighed. Nora just kept chattering.

"You guys remember! Oh . . . but Francie wasn't there. Brook, tell Francie about it! Francie, it was so funny. We went on the teacup ride at the state fair? And I really wanted to go on it. But I had eaten a bunch of cotton candy. A huge bunch."

Ugh! Brook tuned the conversation out. Nora was chattering away, and Francie was giggling along with her. There was no room for Brook to say a word!

That was why Brook daydreamed. In her mind, she could do all sorts of things! And since she was the one thinking it all up, nobody could interrupt her.

Inside her mind, Brook went back to one of her favorite imaginary places—the comedy club. She'd seen one on TV. She stood on stage with a microphone in her hand and a spotlight on her. Everyone in the audience looked up at her, listening, as she told her jokes

And they laughed!

In the middle of a joke, she noticed a table in the back of the room. Who was that sitting there? It was Darcy and Nora and Francie. All three of them leaned forward attentively.

A glow of satisfaction warmed her. She was telling the story of the teacup ride—only *better*. At last, her friends realized that she could be funny and outgoing, too.

"Hey, Brook! Can you hold the horses?" Darcy asked, breaking into her thoughts.

Brook shook her head and blinked. Darcy was handing her the reins of their horses. Francie was on her back in the snow, wiggling her arms and legs.

"Um . . . what?" Brook asked.

"Earth to Brookie," Nora giggled. "We're going to make snow angels. Can you just hold the reins for a sec? We'll take turns."

Brook climbed off her horse and took the reins of the other horses. She was biting her lips when, suddenly, Francie sat up.

"Are you okay, Brook?" Francie asked.

This is it! Brook thought with a happy little rush. *Finally, they want to know what I think.*

"Well, actually," she began, feeling self-conscious. "I, um . . . I don't mind holding the horses right now. But sometimes I feel like—"

"Like we make you do stuff for us?" Darcy offered.

"Not exactly. It's just that you guys talk so much. And I never seem to have anything to say."

"Well, that's okay!" Nora crowed. "You don't have to *say* anything to us. We've all been friends forever! We always know what you're thinking."

"But that's just it. Sometimes you don't," Brook said, thinking of the attendance monitor situation.

"Sure we do!" Darcy added reassuringly. "Don't worry. Besides, what would you do without us to stick up for you and tell people what's on your mind?"

"Well—," Brook said reluctantly.

"Believe me, Brook. It's not always easy sticking up for yourself!" Nora said. "I'd much rather be in your shoes—with people looking out for me."

"I guess." Brook clutched the reins of the horses as the girls ran off to a fresh patch of snow. She felt all muddled up inside! Maybe she was better off this way. Her friends didn't always get it right, but at least they saved her from having to speak up.

"I'm putting pine cones on mine," Francie announced. "Look, now it's got eyes!"

"Cool!" Nora said. She flopped down in the snow and began flapping her arms like wings. "I never thought of that. Let's make halos out of sticks."

"Stick halos?" Darcy giggled. "I don't think so!"

"I'm done!" Nora squealed. "Let's give mine a nose, too."

The three girls got to work decorating Nora's snow angel. Then Darcy made hers. Then Francie went again! They were creating a million angels—without Brook!

In spite of the chill, Brook felt her face flush hotly with anger. Why wouldn't they listen to her? Why did they pretend to be concerned about her?

They don't care about my feelings, she thought bitterly. *I'm just here to listen to their stories, to hold their horses, to watch their games.*

Enough already!

Brook carefully tied the horses to a tree. Then she turned around and walked away. A few yards into the woods, she turned around and looked back. They were going to notice she was leaving, weren't they?

Nope. They just kept giggling as they started mushing snow together into a snowman.

Well, fine. Brook marched into the woods, letting the forest close behind her. Somewhere in the back of her mind, she remembered Darcy warning her about getting lost in the woods, but she didn't care. She had to get away from her so-called friends.

She crashed through the underbrush, kicking at the snow as she walked. She trudged along until she came to a small clearing deep in the woods, near a rock wall. The sun was beating down, and the rocks blocked the wind. With her snow pants and warm coat, Brook was nice and comfortable.

All right! she thought, settling down on a boulder. *Those guys will never find me here.*

Brook looked around, satisfied. *Just me and these trees . . . these rocks . . .*

A few minutes later, solitude lost its appeal.

If something happened to me here, no one would ever find me, she thought. Plus, it was suddenly getting colder. An icy wind blew at her back, making the hair on her neck stand on end.

Suddenly she heard footsteps behind her, padding through the snow.

Oh great, she thought. *What could be wandering around this deep in the woods?*

Her mind raced over the possibilities: a mountain lion. A grizzly bear that forgot how to hibernate.

Or maybe, just maybe, it was the ghost of the red-eyed wolf!

"Oh! Hi," said a cheerful voice. "What are you doing here?"

Brook spun around. *A girl?*

Blinking, she studied the girl. She was about Brook's age. She had blond hair and an angelic face with a tiny pug nose. She was wearing an old-fashioned coat, made of heavy wool—unlike Brook's puffy down parka. A high, lacy collar poked out under the coat.

"What's the matter?" the girl asked. "Rat got your tongue?"

"Cat," Brook said shyly.

"What?"

"It's cat. Cat got your tongue."

"Oh!" The girl laughed a tinkly, pretty laugh and sat down next to Brook. "Whatever. I guess neither one has your tongue."

"Right," Brook said. Then she lapsed into silence. She had a million questions. What was this girl doing in the middle of the woods? Who was she? Where had she come from? But as usual, she felt too shy to say anything.

"You didn't answer my question," the girl prodded.

"Oh!" Brook searched her brain, trying to remember the question. "What did you ask me?"

Brook blushed. She sounded like an idiot!

But the girl just laughed in a friendly way. "I'm sorry," she said. "It's just that you looked so startled. I hope I didn't scare you!"

She looked so friendly and hopeful. Brook began to relax a little.

"I'm not scared," Brook admitted. "Though it is weird, meeting someone in the middle of the woods."

"Tell me about it! I thought you were a wood sprite or something," the girl said. "I'm playing hooky. We were on a field trip, but I can't stand my school. So I sneaked away."

"I know the feeling," Brook said, nodding. "I was just out riding with my friends, but I got mad and stormed off."

"Didn't they follow you?" The girl looked concerned.

Brook's eyes welled up with tears. "They didn't even notice," she said in a shaky voice.

"What a bunch of stinkers!" the girl exclaimed.

That was it for Brook. The floodgates opened, and tears streaked down her cheeks.

"Oh, please don't cry," the girl said, fluttering around her.

"I'b sorry," Brook mumbled through her tears. "I've just been really biserable."

"Biserable?" The girl cocked her head.

Brook sniffed, then blew her nose loudly. "Miserable," she said more clearly.

"Oh!" The girl clapped a hand over her mouth, masking a giggle.

"What's so funny?" Brook demanded.

"And were you glooby?" the girl teased.

Brook was confused for a second. Then she caught on. She couldn't help but grin.

"I was glooby and biserable. And then—"

"Yes?" The girl looked at her expectantly.

"I was really bubbed!"

The two girls erupted into laughter.

"*Bubbed*? I never heard that one before," the girl said. "But at least you got better. Now you're feeling *barvelous!*"

That set them off again. Brook felt totally at ease, as if she had known this girl for years.

"Oh, stop making me laugh," she said, clutching her stomach. Slowly her breath came back.

"We're just laughing *baniacs!*" the girl added.

"My name's Brook, by the way," she said, holding out her hand to shake.

"I'm Angela," the girl answered. But she kept her hand at her side. She perched on a rock next to Brook.

Why won't she shake? Brook wondered, dropping her hand. She decided to change the subject. "How come you have a field trip on Sunday?" she asked.

Angela shrugged. "The Academy is really strict," she explained.

"The Academy? Where is that?" Brook asked.

"We don't have any private schools in Whiterock."

"Nearby," Angela replied. "In another town."

"Aren't you afraid you'll get in trouble? For playing hooky, I mean?"

"Nah! I don't care." Angela waved her hand dismissively.

Wow, Brook thought, looking the girl over again. *If I ever had the nerve to skip school, I'd probably be too nervous to enjoy it.* Whoever this girl was, she had guts!

"How come your stinky friends didn't notice you were gone?" Angela asked.

"I don't know. They never seem to notice anything about me!" Now that she had had a good cry—and a good laugh—Brook felt herself open up. The words just flooded out as she told Angela the entire story. How Darcy had taken her monitor job in class. How her friends always spoke for her.

"I just feel like a big, silent *houseplant*. They listen to Fiona more than they listen to me!"

"Fiona?"

"Darcy's cousin. She's only six, but she talks a lot, and everyone listens. I never get to say a word."

"Oh boy, I have the opposite problem," Angela groaned. "I can never shut up. Everybody's always telling me to pipe down. But I can't help it if I'm smarter than they are."

Brook laughed in spite of herself. "I wish I was that sure of myself," she said.

"Plus, my school is so boring and strict. I hate it!" Angela went on.

"You should come to my school," Brook said. "It's not that bad."

"I wish," Angela said gloomily.

Suddenly, a call echoed from the distance. "Brook! Where *are* you?"

Brook stood up. "They finally noticed I was gone," she said. "I guess I'd better go. My feet are getting cold, anyway."

"Wait!" Angela stood up. "It was fun talking to you. Why don't you come back tomorrow and we'll do something together?"

"Really?" Brook's eyes opened wide. Someone wanted to hang out with her? *Just her?*

"Yeah! I can't stand the little goody-goodies at my school. You're real. And funny," Angela said.

Funny? "Okay," Brook said, beaming. "I'll meet you here tomorrow, after school."

"Wonderful!" Angela said.

Brook nearly floated toward the meadow where her friends were. *Angela thinks I'm funny,* she thought excitedly. *She wants to hang out!*

Just as she got to a bend in the path, she turned around to wave. She felt that chill on her neck again as she lifted her hand. But Angela was gone!

That's weird, she thought as she moved down the path. A second ago, she'd been standing in the middle of the clearing.

Brook laughed to herself. "Maybe she knows some kind of disappearing act!"

"I love this part of Christmas," Darcy announced the next day. School was over, and Darcy, Nora, and Brook were heading down the main stairs.

"I wish every day could be Tree Day," Nora said.

"Are we going to make new ornaments this year?" asked Darcy.

Brook tagged along behind them. She'd forgotten that today was Tree Day.

"There's Francie!" Darcy said, pointing to the edge of the school lawn. "I told her to meet us here. We'll have to hurry if we're going to get to the tree sale before everybody else."

Nora and Darcy hurried away from the building. Brook just stood on the steps uncertainly. She wanted to go with her friends. But she had a *new* friend now. Angela really seemed to like her, and she was waiting.

Brook didn't know what to do.

"Yo, Lauer!" Darcy called back. "Aren't you coming?"

"Um . . ." Brook took a step after her friends. But then she remembered how much fun she'd had with Angela. And she imagined herself sitting silently while Darcy, Nora, and Francie chattered around her.

"No," Brook finally answered. She hiked up her backpack and stared at the ground. She didn't want to see their faces. "I have plans," she explained weakly.

"You have *what*?" Darcy asked.

"Why didn't you tell us?" Nora demanded.

"What kind of plans?" Darcy probed. "A dentist appointment? A visit to Grandma's house?" she teased.

Nora snickered.

Brook felt stung. "I'm meeting a friend," she said, setting her jaw. "I have to go."

"Brook, what are you talking about? It's Tree Day!" Nora was aghast.

Ever since they were little, the girls had had their own Christmas tree, just for the three of them. They put it up at Darcy's house and decorated it themselves. And each year they placed their presents for one another under their special tree.

"We always pick out our tree together," Nora went on. "And this is the first year we get to go alone. Without our parents. And with our own money."

"No more kidding around, Brook," Darcy ordered. "Come on, let's go!"

"I can't," Brook said. She turned her back on the amazed bunch and walked away.

"Brook?" Darcy called after her.

But Brook didn't answer. She couldn't even let herself look back. Sure, she loved Tree Day. But why didn't they understand that she had places to go, other people to see?

I don't have to be a quiet little tagalong! she thought as she trudged toward the edge of town. *I have a personality!*

It took about twenty minutes to reach the outskirts of town. Then she had to tromp through the snow-covered forest until she got to the secluded spot. It was tough to find—but she recognized it when she got there. The clearing . . . the sheer rock with the cave opening. Yup, this was the place.

And there was Angela!

She was sitting on a black log, her eyes closed, letting the brilliant sun warm her face. When the light hit her, her skin looked especially pale. Almost translucent. For a second, Brook thought she could see right through the girl's skin as the light wavered. . . .

She blinked. Just a trick of light!

"Hey!" she called out, approaching Angela.

"Hey, yourself," Angela answered with a grin. "I thought you'd never get here!"

The two girls huddled on the log. Brook looked at her own legs, encased in warm, snow-repellent pants, then glanced at Angela's. She was wearing flimsy long johns and clumpy lace-up boots.

"Oh my gosh! Aren't you freezing?" Brook asked.

Angela just shrugged. "I don't even feel it," she said. "These tights are really warm."

"If you say so," Brook said. She began packing snow into a fort as Angela watched.

"So, how was school today?" Angela asked.

"Okay, I guess," Brook replied. "My friends were weirded out that I was gone for so long yesterday. They kept asking me where I went." She smiled at her new friend. "I didn't tell them anything about you. I just let them wonder. And it killed them that I had somewhere to go today."

She didn't add that she felt a little bad about missing Tree Day.

"What kind of stuff do you do at your school?" asked Angela.

"School stuff," Brook answered, molding a tower for her fort. "Reading and math and history. And science class."

"Science?" Angela asked quizzically.

"You don't have science class?"

"Not really," Angela said hastily. "I told you my school was boring! What do you do in science class?"

"Weird stuff. Sometimes there are dead things, like moths and butterflies. Once we got to pet a real snake." Brook shivered. "Gross."

Angela's blue eyes were filled with curiosity. "What do you mean?"

"You know. That stuff is kind of yucky. Don't you think?"

"Oh. Yeah, I guess I do." Angela gave a little

shiver exactly as Brook had done. "Gross. Moths and snakes. And that's your lunch?"

"Lunch? No! It's science class!" Brook laughed. "Oh, I get it. That's a joke, right?"

Angela's face puckered in confusion, but she nodded. "Right! Just a joke."

Brook kept concentrating on her fort.

"Sooo," Angela said. "Have you ever had bubble gum?"

Brook looked up. "What do you mean? Have I ever tasted it?"

"Yeah. What is it like?"

"It's . . . really sweet, and it tastes like . . . like the color pink. Why? Are you allergic?"

"No. I've just never had it."

Never had bubble gum! Poor Angela. "That Academy must be really strict!" Unless this was another one of her strange jokes.

"Did you ever go to California?" Brook asked, trying to keep the conversation going. "I went last Thanksgiving to see my aunt and uncle."

"No, I've never been there. Did you drive?"

"We flew on a jet."

"Oh!" Angela sounded surprised. "Why didn't you take a magic carpet?"

Brook looked up, and her fort tumbled to the ground. "You have a strange sense of humor."

"I do?" Angela asked.

"That crack about moths and snakes for lunch. And never tasting bubble gum? And magic carpets? Too weird." She laughed. "You're one strange chick."

"Like a chicken?" Angela looked baffled.

"Chick. You know, like a babe."

Angela stood up and put her hand on her hips. "I'm not a baby!"

"Of course not!" Brook insisted. "It's just . . . just what people say."

Angela sighed forlornly. "I guess I may as well just tell you," she said.

"Tell me what?" Brook cocked her head.

"Well, it's going to sound crazy. Maybe I'd better *show* you."

Brook shrugged. "Okay, show me."

Angela stood up and gave Brook a sheepish grin. Then she took a deep breath, squared her shoulders, and walked across the clearing . . .

Right through a tree!

Brook clapped wildly. "Wow, that was pretty cool," she said. "It looked like you really walked through that tree! Are you with the circus? Is that why you made all those weird jokes?"

Angela rolled her eyes. "You don't get it! Look. Watch carefully!"

Angela fixed her eyes on Brook's and stared. Brook began to feel a chill, just like when she'd first met Angela. Something strange was happening . . . but she didn't know what.

She couldn't look away from Angela's eyes. She tried, but it was as if her neck was made of wood—it wouldn't turn away. And her eyes were transfixed.

Amazed, she stared as the girl's eyes became even more blue. At first, they were the color of the sky. But as Brook watched, they became darker and darker.

Soon they looked like the deep blue of marbles in front of a bright light. Then they began to glow, like the blue center of a fire.

All of a sudden, Brook noticed Angela's skin. It was becoming paler as her eyes became brighter. Angela was as white as the snow that surrounded her. Then Brook began to see something. Trees? Pine cones? Angela's form wavered as if she were under water. Then Brook realized the truth.

She was seeing *through* Angela.

A moment later, Angela disappeared completely, except for her two burning blue eyes.

"Angela?" Brook reached out to touch her friend, but her arm wafted through the air. Her heart began to beat wildly.

Suddenly, Angela appeared again. She looked as solid as she had before . . . as solid as a real girl. But Brook knew what she had just seen.

"Do you get it?" Angela asked, the glow fading from her eyes.

"I don't . . . I mean . . ." Brook's nerves were on edge. She backed against the trunk of a tree and clutched the bark with shaking fingers. Somewhere in the back of her mind she remembered that she was miles away from anyone else. Any other *people*.

"I mean, I *think* I get it," she said. "Are you . . . I mean, are you actually . . ."

Angela nodded. "You guessed it. I'm a ghost!"

"Brook, come on. Don't freak out!" Angela called. "It's okay, I'm not going to hurt you. Come out from under that bush, please?"

Brook's heart was thudding a million miles a minute! How had she gotten herself into this?

She wasn't just sitting in the woods with a new friend. She was hanging out with a spirit . . . an apparition . . . a visitor from the great beyond! She thought of the phantom cat-lady from Darcy's ghost story and shivered.

"Leave me alone, Angela," Brook wailed. "Just disappear again. I want to go home!"

"Brookie, don't be scared of me! Come on. We were having a fun time, right? If I wanted to cause you any harm, I would have just done it! I wouldn't have *told* you I was a ghost."

Brook was holding her mittens tightly over her ears, but she could still hear everything Angela said. As she sat huddled in a ball, she thought about this last piece of information.

It was true. Angela had been alone with her

yesterday, and nothing bad had happened. In fact, they'd had a lot of fun!

Brook opened her eyes and peered out at Angela. Right now the ghost girl looked just like anyone else. She cracked jokes and liked to have a good time. In fact, she was livelier than a lot of kids—real kids—that Brook knew.

"Come on out," Angela begged. "I've got an idea for something really fun we can do."

Brook took a deep breath. *Okay, so your new buddy is a ghost,* she told herself. *But she's been cool so far. Maybe you should give her a chance.*

She scrambled out from beneath the bush and gazed at Angela curiously. Now it all made sense! Angela dressed like a kid in an old photograph. And there was a good reason for that. She *was* a kid from the old days. Or at least, she was the ghost of a kid. A kid who lived long, long ago.

"You're not going to hurt me?" Brook asked in a shaky voice.

"Honestly, Brook! Quit being such a nervous Nellie. You're my only human friend! Why would I want to hurt you?"

"And you're not going to scare me, either?"

"You're frightening yourself better than I ever could!" Angela laughed. "Come on, relax. Chill out!"

Brook managed a little smile. She felt pretty brave, making friends with a ghost and everything. Darcy never did anything like this, that was for sure!

"Well?" Angela pressed. "Are you ready to stir up some fun?"

"Maybe," Brook said, and Angela clapped her hands happily. "But first, tell me what your big idea is."

Angela gave her a toothy grin. "You're going to help me shake up the Academy."

"The Academy?" That's right—Angela had talked about her school, and how much she hated the kids there. But what kind of school would a ghost go to?

Angela nodded. "The *Poltergeist* Academy."

"Wait a minute. Are you talking about some kind of school just for ghosts?" Brook asked. "Now I *know* you're kidding me!" She shook her head.

"I'm serious! Cross my heart and hope to die!" Angela said, making a little X on her chest.

Brook squinted at her. "You *are* dead."

"Well . . . whatever." Angela shrugged. "We're supposed to go to school to learn how to be good little haunters. It's totally stupid, but it's true!"

"And you want me to go there with you? To a whole school full of ghosts?" Brook shook her head. "You're one thing, Angela. But a whole bunch of you is *way* too creepy!"

"I've got it all figured out," Angela insisted, shaking her head. "Most of the ghost kids are afraid of humans. If you showed up there, they'd be petrified! There's nothing for you to worry about. You just give 'em a scare! I'll have you out of there before they even realize what's happening."

"They're scared of *humans*?" Brook couldn't believe it.

"Sure!" Angela held her arms out as if it were the most natural thing in the world. "You were scared of me, weren't you?"

"Yeah . . . but ghosts are scary!"

"Not if you're a ghost. If you're a ghost, then humans are scary."

It made sense. Brook's mom had always told her not to be scared of bugs. "You just scared that spider half to death," Mom had pointed out. "All it knows is that a giant human is making all kinds of noise!"

Brook was scared of ghosts because she didn't know any. And if a ghost kid had never met a human . . . he'd probably be scared, too.

"Anyway," Angela continued, "you can help me give the Academy a good scare. And then I'll help you."

"Help me? With what?"

"Come on, Brook." Angela draped herself over the lower branches of a tree and rolled her eyes. "Remember everything we talked about yesterday? Your friends ignore you. Your teacher barely notices you. Your life's a mess! That's why you were wandering around in the woods by yourself."

"Oh, that." Brook sat on a fallen log and looked at her toes. "I don't know. I hate to rock the boat."

"What are you, nuts?" Angela squeaked. "You were really upset yesterday! And I can make everything better for you. I'm sure of it!"

Brook cocked her head at Angela. She sounded so positive! "Well . . . what do you want to do?"

Angela's eyes sparkled as she faced Brook.

"Watch carefully." She swept her arm over a patch of snow. Her fingers scraped into the ground, but the snow remained smooth.

"There's no trail," Brook observed.

"Right!" Angela said. "I don't have a body. I'm a spirit, right? So I can't do a lot of the stuff you do."

"I get it. You can't grab stuff, or pick anything up, because you don't have a body."

"Bingo. So what I want to do is . . . borrow yours."

"You want to borrow my *body*?"

"Right!" Angela grinned. "I'll put myself inside your skin. I'll move your arms, control your legs, and make you talk!"

"You want to borrow my body?" That was totally, completely, *unbelievably* creepy! Brook thought of how Sam's little sister Fiona always wanted to borrow his baseball hat. It bothered Sam, even though Fiona never let anything happen to it. It was *his* baseball hat.

And this was *Brook's* body!

"No way!" she said firmly.

"Don't make up your mind yet," Angela said, holding up her hands. "Just think about it this way. I've been hanging out with you, and I already know you're funny and smart."

"You do?"

"Yes! And if your friends don't know that, it's because you've been too shy to show them. All you need is a little help with your nerves."

"You mean, like standing up for myself?"

Brook asked, thinking of how she had tried to talk to her friends. She just wasn't able to make them understand.

"Right! I'll give you the guts you need. I'll show you how much fun it is to stick to your guns!"

Brook had to admit, Angela's plan was pretty slick. Almost like the kind of thing Darcy would come up with! She'd get to see what a ghost school was like. She'd get to play a prank. And then Angela would come back to Whiterock with her and help her show everyone what the *real* Brook was like!

I can see it now, Brook thought. That obnoxious Jay Greenberg would come up to her with his eyelids flipped back, arms out, groaning like Frankenstein. And instead of shrieking and running away, Brook would say something that would stop him cold.

Jay would be the one left speechless!

Or Annabel Mackinac would walk past her with her snobby friends and make some mean crack about Brook. But this time, Brook wouldn't think of a comeback five minutes later. She'd zing Annabel on the spot!

Brook would finally be able to talk back to people the way Darcy and Nora did. She'd be assertive, talkative—the life of the party! Just like she'd always imagined.

It would be perfect!

"I can't believe I'm saying this, but it sounds great," she said, flushed with excitement. "Except that stuff about jumping inside me."

"It's no big deal," Angela said coyly. "I can hop into you now—just for five minutes—so you can see what it's like."

"Well . . ." Brook hesitated.

"Hey, if you don't want to, that's okay," Angela said, putting her hands on her hips. "No biggie."

"Really?" Brook looked up.

"Sure! I'm sure I could find someone else to do my plan with me."

Brook's heart sank to the ground. She was going to lose her friend because she didn't have the nerve to try something new!

"I'll do it," she said hastily.

"Great," Angela said. "Five minutes, I promise." And the pretty little wraith disappeared.

"Angela? Where are—*oh!*" Brook squeaked.

Something felt very strange!

Her whole body was flooded with energy, like when something scared her and she felt her heart pumping fast. Except this feeling wasn't scary. It was cool!

Brook blinked, astounded. Everything looked different. She realized that she was seeing things the way Angela did!

Brook raised her hand in front of her face and looked at it. She clenched her fist, then stretched her fingers wide.

Hang on a sec, Brook thought. *Who's moving my hand?* Then she realized what was going on: Angela was in control now. She was the one making the moves!

"Wheee-haw!" she called out and turned a perfect cartwheel in the snow. The cold felt delicious and exciting. Then she ran up to the nearest tree and began scrambling up the branches.

"Be careful!" Brook said out loud, breathlessly. She never climbed trees! She was too afraid of falling.

"Relax," Angela's voice echoed in her head. "You'll see! It's really fun."

Finally, she reached the top of the tree. "Okay, now look," Angela told her.

Brook opened her eyes. She tried to cling to the trunk of the tree, but Angela just hung on loosely, letting the wind run through their hair.

"Relax," Angela insisted. "If you hold on any tighter, you're going to strangle the tree!"

Slowly, Brook began to enjoy herself. In the distance, she could see Whiterock, covered in snow like a Christmas card village. She could see the jagged treetops. Birds peered curiously at her, wondering what she was doing up so high.

"Wow," she finally breathed. "It is really cool up here."

She heard Angela laugh. "See? I told you."

"But don't jump out of me and leave me stranded!" Brook added hastily, peeking at the long climb down.

"Don't worry! I'd never do that to you," Angela soothed. To Brook's relief, they began clambering down the tree. Soon her feet were planted on solid ground.

"Wow," was all Brook could say. Her body

began to cool as that electrifying energy faded away. A second later, Angela appeared beside her.

But the pretty little wraith looked tired. She was paler and much more transparent than before. Her image was wavering, and Brook could almost make out the bright berries on the holly bush behind Angela.

"Are you okay?" Brook asked.

Angela sat down on the ground and gave Brook a wan smile. "I'm exhausted," she explained. "That really takes a lot out of a ghost!"

"Anything I can do?" Brook asked sympathetically, sitting next to her friend.

"I'm okay," Angela assured her. "But what did you think?"

"I thought it was great," Brook gushed. "At first it was weird. But once I got used to it, it felt awesome! I would never have climbed up there by myself. But once I was there, I loved it!"

Angela was wide-eyed. "Does that mean . . . ?"

"I'll go along with your plan!" Brook declared. "It sounds like fun."

"Fun?" Angela gave an excited yelp and spun around in a circle. Brook couldn't help but laugh at the ghost girl's enthusiasm. And she felt a little excited, too.

"Brook, *fun* isn't the word," Angela hooted breathlessly. "It's going to be a blast! We're going to turn the Academy upside down—and scare the socks off every ghost under the age of *five hundred!*"

"Wow! I had no idea this was here," said Brook.

Did anybody know about this little town, just through the sparkling cave in the woods? "That must be a heck of a shortcut! I've never heard of any towns this close to Whiterock. What's it called?"

Angela muttered something under her breath.

"What? Mustardville?" Brook shook her head. "Never heard of it. Is it near Big Moose?"

"Would you hurry it up? And stay on the path," Angela insisted. She looked around nervously. "We can't waste any time."

They were following a wooded path. They'd just passed a clear, turquoise pond that Angela had called Glitter Lake. And before that, Brook had noticed a cluster of ice huts in the woods.

"What's the hurry?" Brook asked. She was trying to keep up with Angela, but there was so much to see.

"Duh, Brook! I'm playing hooky, remember?" Angela's eyes flashed impatiently. "If anyone from the school sees me, I'm done for!"

"Oops! Sorry." Brook picked up the pace. "I

didn't realize you had classes this late in the day."

"There's always a class going on at that prison." Angela flashed her a mischievous grin. "I'm going to be dead meat when they find out I've been ditching school. That's why I want to make sure we get to do this prank first!"

"Ugh! Don't say that," Brook said, shuddering.

"What?"

"Dead meat." Brook grimaced. "Remember, I'm going to a ghost school for the first time!"

Angela laughed and started to say something else, but Brook didn't hear it. She was a few paces behind, peering through the trees.

"Hey, wait. Isn't that a pyramid?" she asked. "I've never seen anything so . . . Is it a museum?" The huge stone structure loomed in the distance, surrounded by a sea of . . .

"Sand?" Brook squeaked, stepping through the trees. "How come there's no snow?"

"Yeah, there's some strange stuff in this town," Angela said, dismissing the pyramid with a wave. "Some old guy brought that here. He melts the snow away with some kind of underground heater."

"He must be a pretty weird guy," Brook commented, gazing at the massive stone structure. "How old is he?"

"Ancient. Like five thousand years," Angela said.

"Five thousand years!" Brook laughed. "Girl, you have got to stop exaggerating."

Angela just smiled mysteriously. "I'll show you

the rest of the town later. Right now we've got to get to the Academy!"

With a glance at the golden sand dunes, Brook moved on. As she fell into step beside Angela, she mulled it over. She'd never heard of a pyramid in the woods before! What *was* this strange place?

Suddenly Angela caught her breath. Her eyes went from excited to panicked. "Quick, hop inside that old tree," she said.

"But what—?"

"Quick!" In an instant, Angela zapped herself into a thin column of smoke and slipped into the crevice of a tree.

Brook searched the path. She didn't see anything strange. But she heard what had made Angela so scared.

Footsteps.

Whoever was coming down the path might catch Angela! Brook's heart thudded in her chest. Quickly, she slipped into the tall, hollow tree trunk and scrunched down as far as she could.

The air seemed thick with fear as the footsteps grew louder. From her spot, Brook couldn't see much—just the ground near the path. She squeezed her eyes shut as the footsteps approached and scraped to a halt. Someone was standing a few feet away from her!

Forcing herself to open her eyes, she saw a pointed black shoe edging along the path. A man's shoe!

Had he seen them? Was he going to yank her out of the tree?

"How strange," the man murmured. "I could have sworn I smelled blood. *Human* blood."

Wh-wh-what did he say? His words were like ice in Brook's veins. What kind of guy sniffed out blood?

Pressing her face toward the edge of the hollow, Brook caught a glimpse of him.

Her stomach wrenched at the horrible sight.

It wasn't his black jacket or purple pants that scared her. And she didn't even mind his slicked back hair. But his eyes glowed red. And his teeth . . .

She could have sworn those were fangs hooking over his pale white lips.

That man looked exactly like a hungry, blood-sucking . . .

Vampire!

Inside the hollow of the tree, Brook shivered uncontrollably. She was sure the whole tree was shaking! But she couldn't help it.

A vampire was trying to sniff her out for dinner!

Fear crackled in the air as she tried to calm down. *Think good thoughts! Count backward! Pretend you're somewhere else!*

"Perhaps I was wrong," the man muttered. His feet shifted on the path, moving out of sight.

Brook's heart was still drumming in her ears when she heard the guy give the air a final, deep sniff. Then, slowly, his footsteps faded as he finally walked away.

"Phew!" Angela gave a sigh of relief as she flitted out of the tree and reappeared on the ground near Brook.

"Angela, what—"

"Don't even ask," the ghost said, holding up her hands and rolling her eyes. "He's some kind of rock star. The guy is a total freak."

Brook crawled out and put her hands on her

hips. "A rock star who sniffs out blood?" she insisted. "And did you see those fangs?"

"I know," Angela said, nodding. "A total nut case. What can I tell you?"

Something to make me stop shivering, Brook wanted to say. Instead, she just brushed off her jacket and followed the ghost girl down the path.

🦇   🦇   🦇

"The Academy isn't far now," Angela said when the wooded path turned into a narrow cobblestone street.

Brook was glad. She wanted to get this ghost visit over with!

The street led into a misty village. Soon the girls were hemmed in by old, gray buildings, mostly made of stone. Each building had a large wooden door and several tall, narrow windows.

As they walked, the girls were surrounded by a dense, wispy fog. And the blue sky had turned suddenly to the color of watery milk. When Brook turned to look at the woods behind her, all she saw was a thick, swirling mist.

Brook thought the place looked strangely familiar, even though she was sure she had never been anywhere like this. It looked like another country or something.

That was it! It looked like old London! Brook had seen pictures of the English city in her history books. This street could be a little piece of it!

"This is so cool," Brook said. "It's like one

of those old movie sets that Annabel Mackinac is always talking about!"

"Something like that," Angela said. "But *that's* where we're going."

Brook's eyes followed Angela's pale finger to a dark, forbidding building. It was set back from the street in a little courtyard and surrounded by a spiked, black iron fence.

The dark, twisted letters above the gate spelled out: MISS PRIM'S POLTERGEIST ACADEMY.

"That's your school? It looks like a prison!" Brook said indignantly. "No wonder you wanted out."

"You don't know the half of it," Angela sighed. "This place is a factory. They just want to churn out identical little ghosts. Not individuals. No imagination allowed!" She marched through the gate with grim determination. "It's going to be fun, shaking up this old dump."

"What are we going to do in there, anyway?" Brook asked as she opened the gate. "You never explained the whole plan. Are you going to jump into me and run around yelling and screaming?"

Angela grinned. "Nothing so ghoulish. First, let's make sure everybody in there is occupied. They should be in gym class right about now."

"Gym class?" Brook mused as they sneaked up to the door. "What kind of gym class would ghosts go to?"

But Angela was too excited to answer. "Go ahead, open it—but keep quiet!" Angela whispered.

Brook reached up, grasped the huge brass

knob in the middle of the door, and pushed with all her might.

The door gave a quavery creak as it swung open. A sliver of weak light pierced the gloom of the cavernous hall. Angela slipped through the door and Brook followed, shoving the massive door closed behind them.

It shut with an ominous boom. The two girls held their breath, waiting to see if anyone had heard. Then Brook took a long look around.

The floor of the foyer was covered by a dusty, dark red oriental rug. A glass chandelier hung above them, clanking eerily in the drafty breeze that kept the room at a bone-chilling temperature. A wide staircase stood off to the right, but the top of it was hidden in murky shadows. There were several tall windows covered with thick black draperies. A few dusty mirrors stood along the walls, and an empty fireplace gaped to their left.

"Okay," Angela finally whispered. "We're undetected. Let's go see what they're doing."

Brook followed Angela to a paneled door under the stairs. Angela walked right through it! Brook had to pry it open to follow.

They crept down a few rickety steps and peeked past some rotten boards into the basement.

An old, wrinkled woman stood in the front of the room. Luckily, her dark, deep-set eyes were looking at the rows of empty desks before her. She'd never see the girls at the top of the stairs.

"That's Miss Prim," Angela whispered.

"Cranky old bat. Thinks the whole world needs a good spanking."

The woman was reed thin and dressed in a stiff gray gown. Her hair was pulled into a tight bun and a pair of steely gray glasses was perched on her nose.

"All right now!" Miss Prim announced to the desks. "Ready? Begin!"

On cue, the desks flew into the air, swaying around to the sound of her voice.

"Up! And *left* and center—and *right*—and center—Twirrrrl! And down."

Brook didn't get it. Were the desks haunted? Were they dead desks? Finally the mysterious items of furniture came to rest gently on the ground.

"That was very good," Miss Prim announced. "I can see that we'll soon be able to move on to heavier items, such as dining room tables. Every good ghost should be able to move a dining room table!"

A happy cackle twittered through the room.

"What was that?" Brook whispered, but Angela just shushed her.

Miss Prim gave a satisfied sigh. "All right. Now become visible, and we'll take turns rattling chains and rapping at the windows."

While Brook watched, the air behind each desk wavered for a second. Then a kid appeared in each place. *But not regular kids,* Brook thought with a chill. Ghost kids!

In front of the class was a boy about Brook's

age. He wore short pants that only came down to his knees.

Two little girls stood next to him, with matching blond hair and satiny dresses that reached the ground. They both wore pretty gold bands around their heads.

As Brook watched, more kids began to appear. There was a tall, dark-haired boy in a straw hat, ragged clothes, and bare feet. Another kid was dressed in rich African fabrics, like some kind of prince. But Brook could see that his face was smeared with a pasty white chalk. And a tiny Asian girl tottered along behind him, wrapped in a tight silk kimono.

Other kids kept popping into view. They all walked obediently to the heavy sea chest in the corner. The spunky boy in the short pants was handing out metal chains. The kids chattered to one another, just like the kids in Brook's classroom.

But this wasn't Brook's classroom.

These kids had shadowed eyes . . .

And transparent skin . . .

And watery images.

There was no denying it.

Brook was sitting in a room full of ghouls!

"Come on," Angela whispered. "Let's go." She backed up the stairs and out the door.

Brook followed her, closing the door with a groan.

"What's the matter?" Angela asked, cocking her head. "You look like you've just seen a ghost!"

"Ha ha," Brook muttered weakly.

"Don't be scared!" Angela said reassuringly. "I promise you, those guys are nothing to be afraid of!"

Brook took a deep breath. "Sorry," she said. "It's just that one ghost is fine. A whole room of them is overwhelming!"

"Don't worry," Angela said. "They'll be busy down here for at least another hour. Meanwhile, we've got to get to work!"

Angela gestured to Brook to follow her up the wide wooden staircase. On the second floor, Angela paused at the door of an old, forgotten closet.

"Would you open the door, please?" she asked Brook.

"I don't get it. Why can't you open doors and stuff?" Brook asked.

"I explained it to you already!" Angela reached for the doorknob, but her hand went right through it. "Remember? That's why I need to borrow your body."

"But the other kids were moving their desks and—"

Angela waved her hand. "All that hard work and practice! I can't be bothered. Not when I've got a buddy like you to help me!"

A buddy like you. It was so nice to have a friend who appreciated her! Brook beamed as she opened the closet door. Inside, under the cobwebs, was a broom, a bottle of oil soap, a mop, and some old rags.

"This just has cleaning supplies," Brook pointed out. "Wrong closet!"

"*Right* closet," Angela retorted, crossing her arms and raising an eyebrow.

"I don't get it," Brook said. "We're going to clean the house? What's so scary about that?"

"Are you kidding?" Angela threw her hands in the air. "Brook, did you see those kids? They're *ghosts.* You know, like *whoooooo!*" She wiggled her fingers and waved her arms. "They live in shadow. They hide in cobwebs. They thrive on dust and gloom. We're going to make this place spotless! It'll drive them *crazy!*"

Angela's eyes sparkled like two little sapphires.

Brook remembered the dank basement where the kids were practicing their ghost antics. Would those creepy little ghosts flip over a clean house?

It was worth a try.

"Let's unmake a mess!" Brook giggled.

🦇 🦇 🦇

An hour later Brook was exhausted. This was tough work! She had beaten the dust out of the draperies and pulled them aside, tying them tightly to the edges of the windowpanes.

She'd wiped the windows squeaky clean, so the weak sun would shine through. She'd opened them wide to let in fresh air.

The rug was rolled up and shoved out of sight. The wooden floor had been mopped to a bright shine.

The mirrors sparkled. A cheerful fire crackled in the fireplace. Armfuls of fresh wildflowers were strewn about the great hall. The foyer looked like a cozy country home, ready for a family to return!

"I'm exhausted," Brook announced.

"I'll bet you are!" Angela cheered. She was whipping up tiny tornadoes with her icy cold breath. The whirling air acted like a little vacuum cleaner, sucking up all the leftover dust.

"Hey," Brook said, impressed. "That whirlwind thing is handy. Like a minivacuum."

"Thanks," Angela said, blowing dust out the front door. "And the flowers were an excellent touch. I can't believe you ran all the way back out to the woods to get them!"

"If you're going to do a job, you may as well do it right. That's what my mom always says," Brook pointed out as she gave a mirror a final shine.

"Is she the one who taught you to clean like this?" Angela looked around the hallway distastefully.

"Yup." Brook nodded.

"Yuck. Pretty impressive." Angela gave a little shudder. "I'm grossing myself out!"

"Then I guess our plan is working," Brook said.

The blond ghost grinned. "Thank you so much, Brook. I never could have done this without you. It's one thing to get rid of some dust with my breath. But you really scrubbed everything!"

"I can't wait to see the reaction," Brook answered with a smile.

Just then they heard a clatter from the basement stairway.

"They're coming," Angela whispered, her eyes wide with excitement. "Come on, we'll hide behind the drapes by the door. *Quick!*"

Brook's heart was in her mouth as she raced behind the thick curtain with her friend. She arranged the fabric around her, making sure she could see the basement door. She didn't want to miss anything!

The door flew open and a few of the kids came trooping out as if everything were normal.

But everything wasn't normal. She saw them stop, stock-still. Their gloomy eyes flashed in horror. The raggedy boy and the girl in the kimono grabbed at each other and cringed.

"What—what happened?" the tiny girl said in a scared voice.

Brook could hear the kids behind them on the steps, complaining that they couldn't get past.

"What's the big idea?" the kid in the knickers rasped. "Get movin', already!" He pushed the other kids out of his way and shoved himself through.

"I ain't got all day ta stand on da steps like—" He stopped suddenly. "What da—" His toughness melted as he looked around at his clean, bright surroundings. His chin began to wobble.

"Miss Prim!" he wailed. "Somethin's goin' on up here!"

Angela stifled a giggle behind the drapery. "Ha! I never thought I'd catch Harvey without his attitude," she sniffed.

Miss Prim was still stuck on the basement steps, tangled among the other ghost students. Brook could hear her ordering the kids out of her way.

"Children! I told you to proceed up the stairs. What *is* the matter with you?"

But no one answered. The kids moved out into the foyer and froze, clinging to one another in fright.

"Honestly, when I tell you to go—*oh!*" Pushing into the tidy foyer, Miss Prim let out a sharp cry.

That was all the kids needed to *really* panic.

The littlest ones began to wail loudly. A little girl in a sunbonnet began running around in circles, shrieking. The girl in the kimono backed into a corner. Even Harvey was whimpering.

"Mary! Chung Li!" Miss Prim shouted. "Harvey! Someone, pull the drapes and shut that front door!"

But the kids were too upset to hear her.

"There's people here!" the boy in the straw hat yelled. "Miss Prim, the people must have found us!" He backed away—right into a shiny mirror.

"What—," he stammered, twirling around. Seeing his reflection in the polished glass, he let out a shriek. *"Augh!"*

That set the other ghost kids off even more. Kids bolted under tables. Someone tripped over the rug and knocked over a lamp. The twin girls grabbed at Miss Prim, hiding their faces in her skirts.

"Make the sparkle go away, Miss Prim," one of them begged. "Make it dirty again!"

"It's just like in our castle when the humans moved in!" the other twin sobbed.

"Those are the Chalfant sisters," Angela whispered. "From medieval France. Hid in a castle for seven hundred years before they came here, hardly made a peep the whole time." She gave a mocking laugh. "Little wimps."

Brook turned to look at her friend—but Angela was gone!

"Where'd you go?" Brook whispered, poking at the drapery where her friend had been. "Don't leave me here!"

Suddenly she felt that weird tingling in her fingers and toes, and her heart began beating faster.

Angela had taken over her body again!

With a shock, Brook realized that she was stepping out from behind the draperies and stomping toward the frantic ghosts!

She felt herself begin to panic as Angela pushed her toward the biggest pack of kids. *Angela didn't tell me about this. What now?*

"Ah! Home at last!" Brook yelled, dancing around the foyer. She couldn't believe what Angela was making her do!

The ghost kids whirled around and stared, their eyes wide with horror.

"What are you doing in my house?" Brook barked. "My mommy and daddy bought this place. We live here now!"

A tiny ghost whimpered from behind Miss Prim's skirts.

The teacher narrowed her eyes. "Wait a minute . . . ," she objected.

But Brook was on a roll. She stalked over to Harvey and scowled at him.

"Are you supposed to be scary?" she demanded. "I'm not afraid of you. I don't even think there's any such thing as ghosts!"

Harvey squeezed his eyes shut as the other ghosts gasped. Then he held up his hands and let out a weak ghost-howl. "Whoo?" he moaned, in a tiny voice.

Brook threw her hands up in the air and let out

an exasperated sigh. "I'm terrified," she mocked. "Now *get out of my house!*"

"Y-yeah! Okay!" Harvey burst into tears and raced back down into the basement.

A moment later the other ghost kids crowded after him, howling and crying.

"She's taking our house," someone said.

"They're moving in! We can't stay here any-more!" cried somebody else.

It was hard for Miss Prim to move as the kids bumped around her, scurrying back to the basement.

Miss Prim glared at Brook. "Who brought you here?" she demanded. Then she narrowed her gaze. "Is that Angela?"

"Whoops! I think this is where we make our exit," Brook heard Angela's voice say.

"Come back here!" the teacher shrieked.

"Come on," Angela muttered, pushing Brook toward the door. "We're outta here!"

🦇 🦇 🦇

"That was the best!" Brook gasped, collapsing in a snowdrift. "I didn't know you were going to make me yell at them!"

"Neither did I," Angela said. "It just came to me, and I did it. Do you mind?"

"No way!" Brook answered. "It was so funny. That Harvey kid, trying to howl . . ."

The girls both put their fingers in the air and wiggled them weakly, imitating him. "Whoo?" they repeated, and burst out laughing again.

Although Angela was still recovering, she couldn't stop laughing.

"I still can't believe how scared they were," Brook said, shaking her head.

"Now you know," Angela agreed. "Those poor little ghosties hate humans. That's why they try to scare you away—so they can have their houses to themselves. A lot of them left their homes because humans tried to film them, or ghost busters tried to catch them."

"You don't seem to be afraid of anything," Brook said. "Doesn't anything scare you?"

"Just school." The ghost girl grinned. "Back when I was alive, I was a pretty fearless girl, too."

"When . . ." Brook couldn't tell if she was asking an impolite question. "When was that, exactly?"

"Well, I was born in 1865, while my parents were on their way out here in a covered wagon. This was the Montana Territory then—not even a state."

Brook swallowed hard. She couldn't believe she was talking to someone who came west on a covered wagon! "What was it like?" she asked. "Where did they come from?"

"I don't even know," Angela admitted. "I just remember bumping around in that wagon. Sometimes my dad would look for gold, and sometimes he'd try to be a farmer. Nothing seemed to work out for us."

"That's so sad," Brook said.

"Then my parents decided to really put down roots and try to farm one more time. Some men helped my dad build a cabin. But I kept running around underfoot. I wanted to help, or play hide-and-seek, or whatever." Angela sighed. "My mom had just had another kid, and she was having trouble keeping me in line."

Angela's face looked faraway as she remembered her story. "I got mad because nobody would play with me. Anyway, I packed up my clothes and ran away."

"You *what*? Where did you think you were going to run to?"

"I don't know! I was just so mad. But before I could get very far, I fell into the well they were digging and broke my neck." Angela shrugged. "And that was the end of little old me."

Brook put a hand to her heart. "You broke your neck?"

Angela nodded. "See?" She flopped her head sideways at an impossible angle. "I died instantly. Scraped myself up pretty good, too."

"Quit that!" Brook covered her eyes. "You're freaking me out!"

"Oops! Sorry." Angela straightened her neck again.

"Your parents . . . they must have been so sad!" Brook said thoughtfully.

"They were heartbroken. That's why I stuck around in their cabin. But they all died of smallpox the next winter, so we were together again. Now, *that* was cool."

"What was?"

"We were like a little roving band of ghosts: me,

my parents, and the baby. The four of us together could clear out a house in one night! We haunted that cabin until it got torn down, then we moved on to a bigger house. One time we haunted a restaurant for fifty years straight." Angela shook her head, smiling at the memory. "We were so great."

"Then how'd you end up at the Academy?"

Angela rolled her eyes. "Some people decided it was cool to have a haunted restaurant. They turned it into a tourist trap! People would just wait for us to turn up. No matter how scary we were—they'd just laugh! Sometimes they'd scream, but they weren't terrified. It wasn't any fun anymore. So when my parents heard about the Academy, they thought it would be good for me. Learn some new techniques."

"But you didn't like it," Brook said.

"No way. I want to be with my parents! I'd been haunting for years. And then dumb old Miss Prim wants to take me back to square one and teach me stuff again? Forget it! I'm the one that should be teaching."

"Well, they might be able to show you stuff you can't do," Brook suggested.

"Forget it. I'd rather hang out with you in your town," Angela said firmly. Then she sat up suddenly. "We should get going! I want to get a good look at the place before the sun sets. Then we can figure out what we want to do tomorrow!"

"Cool!" Brook hopped to her feet.

As the two girls headed toward Whiterock, giggling and horsing around, she couldn't help feeling excited. Haunting the Academy had been a blast. But now she was really going to prove herself.

No more quiet, unassuming little me, she thought. *People are going to see that I've got guts. With Angela's help, I'm going to talk more, laugh more, and be more assertive. I'll be a babbling Brook!*

🦇 🦇 🦇

"Oh, gross!" Angela complained as she checked out Brook's room. "No wonder you were so good at cleaning the Academy. This place is spotless!"

"Sorry!" Brook ran her hands over the books that were lined up neatly on a white shelf. A few fuzzy stuffed animals smiled from her bed. Papers were stacked neatly on her desk, and her pens were in a drawer. The wooden floor was swept clean, and a little rag rug was exactly in the center of the floor.

It was a clean room, all right. In fact, the whole Lauer house was kept neat as a pin. Everyone pitched in to keep it that way.

"Well, there's got to be somewhere I can sleep," Angela complained. She squeezed herself through the keyhole in Brook's closet.

"No dust, no must!" her voice floated through the closed door. "Even your shoes are tidy. Do you hang up your socks?"

"No!" Brook laughed. "What about under my bed?"

Angela appeared through the crack under the closet door and shot across the room to the bed.

"Brook, have you ever heard of dust bunnies?

57

They make excellent pets," Angela teased.

"I'm sorry!" Brook said, hiding a grin. It never occurred to her that her neatness would make anyone mad. "You really can't sleep without gloom and grime?"

"Well, at least a cobweb or two," Angela admitted.

"Hmm." Brook screwed up her face and thought for a second. Then she jumped up. "I've got it!" she announced.

Angela followed her out into the hallway. Brook pointed to the ceiling, where there was a pulldown door.

"The attic," she whispered. "It's the creepiest place on earth."

"I'll be the judge of that," Angela said, winking. She flitted up to the trapdoor and squeezed in.

"Well, it's a little better. But these neat stacks of boxes are a little sickening." There was a pause. "I found your summer clothes. Your mom must label everything! Is she the queen of organization?"

"Try the back corners, under the eaves."

"Ahh . . . cobwebs. And some soot from the chimney! That's much better. Pretty cozy!" Angela called down.

"Okay. I'll see you tomorrow, right?"

"Right! Good night, Brook. Sweet screams!"

"What?"

Angela's head appeared through the trapdoor. She gave Brook a joking smirk. "Just a little ghost humor."

Brook shrugged. "Sweet screams, Angela."

"Lunchtime. Finally! I'm starving," Darcy announced the next day.

Brook, Darcy, and Nora were in their usual cafeteria spot, by the window in the corner.

"What's the matter, Brook?" Nora wanted to know.

"Huh?" Brook blinked and turned away from the window. She had been peering out anxiously, searching for Angela.

"You're a million miles away." Nora brushed her dark bangs back and turned toward the window. "What are you looking at?"

"Nobody! I mean . . . nothing," Brook insisted. There was no way she could tell the truth—that she was expecting a ghost!

Where is she? she wondered. When Brook got up that morning, there was no sign of Angela. Was the ghost wimping out on her end of the plan?

"Maybe she's looking for her new friend from yesterday," Darcy said, unwrapping her sandwich. She eyed Brook curiously, checking out her reaction.

Brook's heart dropped. Did Darcy know about

Angela? She turned away from the window.

"The mysterious new friend!" Nora chirped. "Oh my gosh, Darcy, do you have *information* about Brook's secret friend? Tell all! I mean, no offense, Brook, but I'm dying to know. And you won't say a word. Though you don't usually say much, anyway."

"Relax, Nora," Darcy said. She helped herself to a potato chip out of Nora's bag. "I was just kidding."

Brook sighed. She was relieved. If she was going to make her friends believe she had guts, they couldn't know that Brook was getting extra help.

Not to mention that Angela was a ghost! Brook didn't know how she'd explain *that* part.

"Oh, I thought you knew some big secret," Nora said. "Like in that movie we saw? Where the guy had a million dollars and didn't know what to do with it?"

"That was so dumb," Darcy complained. "Like anyone wouldn't know what to do with a million dollars."

"Well, I don't know what I'd do. I'd have to think about it," Nora said.

Darcy and Nora were off and running, chattering about their plans. This was what always happened. They'd go off on some topic, and Brook got stuck listening from the sidelines.

Brook slumped a little in her seat. *I guess Angela's not coming,* she thought. *So much for the new Brook.*

"I wouldn't have to think about it," Darcy announced. "I'd spend the whole million on the ranch. New stables, new saddles. And for me and my mom, a big, heated pool."

"Well, I guess I would buy my mom some stuff, like new clothes." Nora sighed. "Except my mom doesn't care about clothes that much. So maybe I'd just buy her a truck like my dad's."

"I think I'd—," Brook began.

"Another truck?" Darcy broke in, giving Nora a quizzical look. "You already have one."

"She's always borrowing the truck," Nora explained. "She loves it! And Dad complains that he has to drive the hatchback."

As they chattered back and forth, Brook suddenly felt that icy wind—Angela's wind. She looked around for the little blond wraith, but didn't see her.

"Forget about me?" Angela teased.

Then Brook's fingers began to tingle. It was happening!

"I know what I'd do with a million bucks," Brook suddenly said, cutting off the other girls.

Startled, Darcy and Nora went silent.

"First of all, I'd buy all of Fiona's Girl Scout cookies," Brook announced. "That would make her year! Then I'd buy this school."

"Buy the school?" Nora was dumbfounded.

Darcy laughed. "Whiterock Elementary School, on sale now!"

"Why would you buy the school?" Nora wondered.

"So I could close it down!" Brook whooped.

"Permanent vacation! Tear it to the ground and build an amusement park!"

"Tear down the school?" Darcy giggled. "Brook, you love school. You're a bookworm!"

"I am?" Brook was stunned for a split second. "Oh, that's right. That's why I'd put in a big library, too. In the amusement park."

"In the amusement park?" Nora shrieked.

"Sure! You get off the roller coaster, you barf, and you sit down and read about the history of barf."

"Eeeeewwww!" Nora and Darcy squealed.

"Okay. Okay. But that's not even the best part!" Angela was having a great time. Brook felt like she was watching a movie—except she was the star! "I'd install a beach," Brook announced.

"A beach?" Nora squeaked.

"In Montana?" Darcy laughed.

"I'd have some ocean brought in, a little sand. And I'd build it near one of the hot springs so it would be toasty warm. We could all go surfing!"

Angela was rolling along, and Brook was flushed with excitement. She could tell a story! She could make people laugh!

At last, she was the star of the group!

When the bell rang, Brook wasn't sure if Angela was going to make a repeat appearance or not. *Lunch was fun . . . but was that all?* she wondered.

She had her answer almost immediately.

Math was right after lunch. And every day,

Darcy and Nora moaned that it was enough to ruin your appetite.

But Brook didn't mind. She usually got the right answers on tests. And when the teacher did a problem on the board, she scratched it out herself and figured out the answer first. If only she'd get called on once in a while!

Sure, she could raise her hand. But when the time came, she always chickened out. Besides, it would be so embarrassing if she gave the wrong answer!

As the teacher wrote an algebra problem on the blackboard, Brook doodled along. She had the answer in seconds.

"Work on that, and let me know when you've figured it out," Ms. Yellowfeather said.

To her surprise, Brook's hand shot up in the air. "I know! I figured it out already," Brook announced.

"Brook Lauer! My goodness." The teacher looked surprised and pleased. "Well, what is the answer?"

"Thirty-four!"

"Excellent."

Brook glowed with pride. *Thanks, Angela,* she said silently.

"Thank you, Brook. It's nice to have you participating in the class." Ms. Yellowfeather winked and turned back to the board.

"You're welcome, *Penelope*," Brook muttered, calling the teacher by her first name.

The kids around her tittered, and Darcy stared at her, astonished. Brook was shocked. That was such an obnoxious thing to do!

Then again . . . it was funny.

She waited breathlessly to see if Ms. Yellowfeather had heard it, but she just kept on writing on the blackboard. Phew!

"Penelope?" Jay Greenberg whispered. "How'd you find that out?"

"It's right on her grade book, Sherlock," Brook answered.

Jay cracked a wide grin. "Think they call her Penny?" he whispered. "If there's inflation, is she going to change her name to Nickel?" He laughed again.

This time, Ms. Yellowfeather could tell something was up. She turned around.

"Is there a problem?" she asked the class.

The room fell silent.

"That's what I thought," she said, turning back to the board. Which was even funnier, for some reason. The class erupted into giggles.

Ms. Yellowfeather whipped around. "All right! Just what is going on?" she demanded.

Brook was amazed. A few well-placed wisecracks, and the whole class fell apart! It was kind of scary . . . and kind of fun.

Fortunately, Angela kept her mouth shut this time. Ms. Yellowfeather just glared at the class as kids squirmed. After a long moment, the teacher turned back to the blackboard again, and the class was out of danger. No one got in trouble.

But Brook was buzzing with a feeling of power.

She felt Angela leave her body. "See you later, hot shot," the ghost whispered. Then she was gone.

For the rest of the day Brook kept playing those funny scenes in her head. She couldn't believe she had entertained her friends at lunch like that! And answered that math question. And made the whole class laugh!

For once, she was the center of attention. She'd wanted Angela to stick around, but it was okay. The ghost had done plenty for one day.

But the ghost struck again.

The class was just filing out when Brook felt an icy wind at her back.

"Not so fast, Brook!" Angela said. And hopped into her body.

"What now?" Brook whispered.

"Trust me," answered Angela.

Leaning out the door, Brook called to Darcy and Nora. "Hey, guys! I'll catch up with you at the Dairy Saloon!"

Before she could take in her friends' reactions, Brook was tugged back into the classroom. With a shock, she realized she was walking straight to the teacher's desk.

Ms. Yellowfeather was packing up her books and purse. Angela planted Brook's feet firmly in front of the teacher and put her hands on her hips.

Panic turned Brook's body to stone.

What am I doing here?

"Ms. Yellowfeather?"

Brook heard her voice ring out in the silent classroom. But she definitely wasn't doing the talking. This was all Angela's idea, and Brook had no clue what she was up to.

The teacher looked up expectantly. "Oh, Brook! I thought you left with the others. Is there something I can help you with?"

"Yes ma'am," Brook said. "It's about the job of attendance monitor."

"I know," Ms. Yellowfeather said, smiling sheepishly. "I didn't realize you disliked the job so much. I would never have made you do it for so long!"

"That's just the problem," Brook said. "I *liked* the job. I liked it a lot. I was pretty upset when you took it away from me. Did I do something wrong?"

"No! You did the job very well," the teacher answered, confused. "Didn't you say you didn't want to do it anymore? That you wanted Darcy to do it instead?"

"No." Brook struggled to keep the ghost under

control. She wanted to stay polite. "Actually, Nora said I didn't want to do it. Then Darcy jumped in and offered to take over. You never asked me if I wanted to be attendance monitor."

Ms. Yellowfeather sighed. "Brook, I apologize." Her brown eyes were rueful. "You're right. I should have asked you."

Brook felt a glimmer of satisfaction. It wasn't often that a teacher ate her words.

"You know," the teacher went on, "substituting for Ms. Blundell hasn't been easy. When I get something wrong, I want you kids to let me know." She gave Brook a reassuring smile. "As of tomorrow, you've got your job back. Okay?"

"Okay." Brook grinned. "Thank you." And then her feet were walking her right back out of the classroom.

Out in the hall, Angela popped out of Brook's body. She leaned against the wall, weak and a little breathless. But her face was radiantly happy.

"Well? How was that?" Angela asked.

"I can't believe it," Brook said. "This has been the most excellent day! You got Ms. Yellowfeather to actually *apologize* to me. And I got my job back!"

"Not bad at all, if I do say so myself," Angela chirped. She took a few bows, then a deep curtsy.

Brook gave a little clap as they headed toward the double doors. "Now everyone thinks I'm funny and smart," she said. "It's perfect. Thanks, Angela."

"It's just the beginning," Angela responded, skipping down the school steps. "Wait till tomorrow!"

"Tomorrow?" Brook frowned. "Wait. I thought we were just—"

"Don't worry, little Brooksie!" Angela said, rolling her eyes. "I've got it all under control. Wasn't today fabulously fun?"

"Yes," Brook agreed, a little dubiously. She thought they were just spending one day together in Whiterock! What was Angela planning now?

"Well? Don't you trust me?"

"Of course I trust you. It's just that—"

"Can't have too much of a good thing, can you?" asked Angela. Her cornflower blue eyes sparkled in her pale, pretty face. She spread her arms out, waiting for Brook's answer.

Brook bit her lip. Something about Angela made her nervous. This ghost was no angel.

But she couldn't bear to turn her buddy down. Especially since Angela had turned her whole life around!

I've got nothing to be nervous about! Brook thought. *Angela's my friend.*

"You're right," Brook said, smiling. "You can't have too much of a good thing." She reached into her pocket. "And I've got a special surprise for you."

Angela read the wrapper and let out a yelp. "Bubble gum! All right! Let's give it a chew!"

🦇 🦇 🦇

The next morning, Brook wasn't sure what to expect when the first bell rang.

"Yuck, another Wednesday," Darcy muttered. She grimaced as she slid into her desk. "A quiz in the morning, and science in the afternoon."

"And right in the middle of the week!" Nora added. "So you can't look forward to the weekend yet. I hate Wednesdays!"

Brook just nodded. If Angela showed up, today definitely wouldn't be a humdrum day.

As soon as Ms. Yellowfeather took attendance, Darcy was out of her seat like a shot.

"All finished?" she asked. "I'll take the list to the office!"

The teacher gave her a hard look. "There's been a change."

"What?" Baffled, Darcy froze in the aisle.

"When you offered to take the job, there was one person we forgot to consult. That person was Brook."

Darcy looked relieved. "Oh, don't worry, Ms. Yellowfeather. Brook doesn't mind!"

"That's not entirely true. Brook?" Ms. Yellowfeather said inquiringly.

All eyes were on Brook. But the only faces that Brook noticed were Darcy's and Nora's. She gulped. She was so excited about being able to keep the job, she'd forgotten about her friend's feelings!

Brook had to force the words out. "Actually, Darcy, I wanted to keep the job."

Stricken, Darcy sank into her chair.

Brook stared at the floor. She felt like a rat!

"We weren't fibbing or anything, Ms. Yellowfeather!" Nora blabbed in a high voice. "I just thought . . . Brook didn't seem like she wanted to do it. I thought that meant she didn't want to. But I didn't lie about it. I honestly thought—"

"All right, Nora. I understand that." Ms. Yellowfeather held up a hand to quiet Nora. "It's really my fault. I should have consulted Brook. Instead, she had to come to me after school and explain the situation. So Brook is our monitor again. Darcy, we can find another job for you."

Darcy didn't answer. Instead, she slumped further into her chair.

Brook went to the teacher's desk and took the attendance list. But she couldn't ignore the awkward hush over the class. She could feel the kids staring at her. Quickly, she ducked out of the room.

Well, Brook Lauer, you're attendance monitor again, she thought as she walked through the empty hallways. *How does it feel?*

The truth was, it felt terrible.

The excitement was gone now. Instead, her heart was throbbing with guilt. The whole job of attendance monitor was ruined! Now she was stuck with it. Every day, when she took the list from Ms. Yellowfeather, she was going to remember Darcy's shocked face.

Where is Angela? Brook wondered. She wanted her friend to know that things had backfired. Maybe Angela would be able to think of a way to make it better.

At least Brook could warn her not to do her any more favors. From now on, Brook wanted to fight her own battles.

*   *   *

The morning dragged on. Brook felt like she was wearing a cement hat, so heavy that she couldn't lift her head and face her friends.

But when the lunch bell rang, her time ran out. Darcy and Nora cornered her in the cafeteria.

"Why didn't you just say something if you wanted to be the attendance monitor?" Darcy demanded. "Ms. Yellowfeather corrected us in front of the whole class!"

"It was *totally* embarrassing," Nora added.

Brook took a deep breath. "I'm really sorry," she said. "I didn't mean to embarrass you. But you guys are always making decisions for me."

"So why didn't you say something on Friday, when the whole thing started?" Darcy fumed.

Brook shrugged. "I don't know."

"I can't believe you!" Darcy snapped. "I have enough trouble in school without you getting me on Ms. Yellowfeather's bad side!"

Brook blinked in surprise. Darcy didn't usually have a hot temper. "Darcy, wait a minute—"

"No, *you* wait a minute," Darcy interrupted. "The next time you want to go behind my back, do me a favor and warn me first!"

She stormed off. Nora watched her helplessly, then turned to Brook. "I'd better go after her. We can talk about it later." Nora patted Brook on the shoulder. "Don't worry. She'll chill out." Then she went in search of Darcy.

Still clutching her wrinkled lunch bag, Brook sat down at the first table she could find. Unfortunately, she ended up across from Jay Greenberg.

"Uh-oh!" he hooted. "It's Brook Lauer, the renegade attendance monitor!" He held out a pretzel stick as a microphone. "Tell us, Brook. How did it feel to wrestle your job from Darcy and Nora? And what's next for you? Will you go after bigger jobs, like clapping erasers and handing out test papers?"

"Maybe she's hoping to be named class tattletale," Annabel Mackinac suggested from the other end of the table.

Her friends tittered.

"Leave me alone," Brook said. She reached out to the pretzel mike and snapped it in half. "Thanks," she said, biting into it.

Jay blinked in surprise. He'd never seen Brook fight back before. Changing gears, he began aiming potato chips at Annabel's pudding.

That left Brook alone with her guilty thoughts.

This whole thing with Angela was beginning to unravel. Darcy was steaming mad. And if Brook wasn't careful, she'd end up ticking off Nora, too.

I'm going to lose all my friends!

And where the heck was Angela?

Time for an afternoon nap, Brook thought when she saw the battered projector in the classroom. Movies were lots of fun at the cinemaplex. But the films shown at school were usually snooze city.

Settled in her desk, Brook tried to catch Darcy's eye. But Darcy just stared ahead with a stormy look on her face.

Brook turned around, but Darcy sunk her head in her notebook.

Across the aisle, Nora shrugged with a look that said: *Give her time.*

"Settle down, class." Ms. Yellowfeather walked to the front of the classroom and pulled down the screen. "We're going to be watching *The Life Cycle of the Frog,*" she announced.

The class groaned, and Jay Greenberg let out a ribbet.

"The film is a little old, but the facts are still valid," the teacher said. "Take notes as you watch. There'll be a short quiz at the end of the film."

With a collective groan, kids began pulling out notebooks. Brook sat with her pencil poised as the lights went out and the projector began to hum.

"The frog is a fascinating creature," the narrator's voice droned. "Does it have lungs or gills? Is it a creature of land or sea? Is it cold-blooded or warm? These questions will be answered as we observe the frog in all phases of development."

"Oh, this is *deadly*," a voice complained. "It's worse than the Academy!"

Brook looked around. Who was talking? No one else seemed to hear the voice. But Angela was perched on top of the bookshelf next to the pencil sharpener.

"I mean, who writes this garbage?" she demanded. "Do the frogs know about this? Once this gets out, you're going to have a swampful of mad bullfrogs. There'll be a froggy riot!"

Quickly, Brook slipped out of her desk and went over to the pencil sharpener. "What are you doing here?" she whispered. "And how come no one else can see you?"

Angela shrugged. "I only want *you* to see me right now. It's one of the tricks of being a ghostie." She put her hands on her hips. "I can see I'm going to have to liven this class up."

"No. Wait! Angela, I have to talk to you—"

But the perky little ghost had disappeared with a little wiggle of excitement. Suddenly Brook felt that tingle in her fingers and toes.

What was Angela going to do now?

Brook felt herself march back to her desk. Her head swiveled toward the movie screen. It was such a weird feeling, not being in control of her own body. And it was starting to annoy her!

On the screen, a lime green frog flicked his tongue out and snapped a fly into his mouth.

"Mmm, yum!" Brook said in a growly voice. "These school lunches have really improved."

Some of the kids giggled.

Nervously, Brook turned to the back of the classroom. Luckily, Ms. Yellowfeather didn't seem to have heard her.

But Angela wasn't done yet. In the movie, a frog jumped onto another frog and they began fighting.

"Get off my back, Penelope!" Brook squeaked.

A few more people laughed. Jay Greenberg shot a spitball at the screen and it bounced off. Darcy turned around and glared at Brook.

Across the aisle, Nora bristled. "Gee, Brook," she whispered. "Take it easy."

Brook tried to clamp her mouth shut. She screwed her face up tight, trying to hold Angela back. Tears formed in her eyes as the narrator droned on and on.

"Would someone shut this guy up?" Brook demanded. "Shut up, Mister Boring!" she shouted.

In the back of the room, Ms. Yellowfeather stood up.

"Did someone say something?" she asked sharply.

Brook's heart dipped into her shoes. But Angela was too keyed up to even notice that Ms. Yellowfeather was onto her.

A big, warty bullfrog appeared in the movie. "Hey, it's the principal!" Brook squealed.

By now, the whole class was laughing. Other kids were adding to the comments. It was out of control!

"Oh, look. Frogs on parade!" Brook cheered as a line of frogs leaped across the screen.

Suddenly the lights went on and the projector clattered to a halt. The class fell silent.

"All right." Ms. Yellowfeather strode to the front of the room and scowled at the class. There were still a few titters, but some kids looked scared.

"Well? Who's the wisecracker?"

"It was Nora—the old bigmouth!" Brook blurted out. Brook put her hand over her own mouth in horror, but Angela made her snatch it away almost immediately.

"It was *not!*" Nora said.

"It was Brook," Darcy added. She stared at Brook accusingly. "What is the matter with you?"

To Brook's horror, Angela made her stand up and throw her hands out to the sides, dramatically.

"All right! All right! I confess!" Brook cried out. "I did it. I interrupted *The Life Cycle of the Frog*! I'm a terrible person!"

"Brook!" Ms. Yellowfeather looked at her, wide-eyed. "I'm surprised at you."

"But it's true, Your Majesty!" Brook said. "Send me to the chopping block. Off with my head!"

Ms. Yellowfeather put a hand on her hip. "I

don't know why you're acting this way, Brook. But I want it to stop."

"You want me to *shop?*" Brook replied. "What do you need? Celery? New shoes?"

"That's it." Ms. Yellowfeather's mouth was a grim line. "Brook Lauer, report to the principal's office. *Immediately.*"

"The dungeon," Brook muttered. "Fine with me. Nothing could be worse than this boring class." She stalked out of the classroom.

What did I do?

With each step, Brook felt more and more humiliated. All she could think of was the shocked, hurt faces of her best friends. She'd accused them!

And Ms. Yellowfeather! She was having enough trouble, coming in to teach their class halfway through the year. Brook had made it worse!

Angela had really gone overboard!

But the ghost girl was still maneuvering Brook's body, whistling and skipping. She pushed her down the hallway—right toward the front door!

"What are you doing?" Brook asked.

"They sent you out of class," Angela's voice said. "Why not slip out of school completely?"

With a colossal effort, Brook stopped walking. Angela pushed her toward the door, but Brook planted her feet firmly on the floor and wouldn't budge.

"What's the matter?" Angela prodded. "Come on. Let's have some fun!"

"She told us to go to the principal's office," Brook said firmly.

"You want to tell off the principal? Cool!" Angela cheered. "That'll be great!"

"Angela!" Brook was getting mad. "I said you could spice things up. Yesterday was a lot of fun. But now you're going overboard."

"Don't be such a stick-in-the-mud!" Angela scolded. "You're so boring."

"I mean it! I appreciate your help. But now you're getting me in trouble. I'd like to try doing things on my own again."

"But I like it here. Come on, let's go sass the principal."

Brook struggled, but slowly she felt Angela guiding her body . . .

Back toward the principal's office.

"Wasn't it enough that you talked back to Ms. Yellowfeather?" Brook asked.

"That was just the beginning!" Angela exclaimed. "Come on, Brook. This is a blast!"

A *blast*? Hardly!

But Angela was having the time of her life . . . or death. She was skipping happily toward the principal's office, ready to shake up the whole school.

And Brook was going to have to take the blame!

13

"*No!*"

Straining and struggling, Brook finally ground to a halt. She was starting to panic. Angela didn't want to give up control. The little sprite wanted to keep Brook's body.

Somehow, Brook had to get her out of there!

What am I going to do? she wondered as she stood in the hallway of the school. She knew she looked silly. Angela kept moving one leg, and Brook kept moving it back. She was grunting with the effort of keeping her body steady. Anyone who saw her would think she was totally nuts.

At least Angela was due to get tired soon! Then she'd have to pop out and rest. But Brook couldn't take the chance that Angela would have time to tell off the principal before she had to stop for a breather.

Sassing the principal. She could see it all now. Her life at Whiterock Elementary would be over. They'd suspend her. Maybe even send her away to some awful school for young criminals.

She had to get Angela out of her body—fast.

Suddenly she remembered their stunt at the Academy—how they'd grossed the ghosts out by cleaning up the place. *And Angela couldn't stand my squeaky clean room,* Brook thought.

Clean things bugged ghosts. *What if I cleaned up my thoughts?*

While Angela tried to push her ahead, Brook concentrated on thinking clean.

She remembered what it was like to scrub away the grime and dirt at the Academy. Everything had looked so bright and shiny once it was polished. . . .

"Hey!" she heard Angela shout.

She screwed up her face and focused again. She thought of how she helped Darcy sweep out the horse stables so everything was neat as a pin. She could almost hear the horses make their contented little noises as the girls brought in fresh hay.

"Ugh! Quit that," Angela warned her.

Wow! This must be working, Brook thought.

She switched her thoughts to doing the dishes. She always wiped the plates squeaky clean and stacked them neatly by the sink.

With a final push, Brook imagined herself in a hot, steamy bubble bath, covered with lather. She wiggled her toes in the hot water and watched her rubber duck bobbing on the surface, dodging bubbles. She could almost feel her fingers getting wrinkled!

"All right, forget it," Angela snapped. "I'm out of here."

Brook sagged as her body returned to normal.

A second later, Angela appeared next to her, eyes blazing. "Boy. Somebody's in a bad mood! Why don't you just slap me in the face?"

"I'm sorry. But you wouldn't listen to me," Brook explained. "I told you that things were getting out of hand. I don't want to have any more adventures!" She heaved a big sigh. "I have enough on my hands trying to fix up the ones we've already had."

"Oh, come on! You're not really upset about this stuff, are you?" Angela was amazed. "Who cares what a couple of humans think?"

"Angela, those *humans* are my friends!" Brook sighed. "Look, I appreciate everything you tried to do. But this kind of fun—it's just not my style! From now on, let's just hang out together outside of school. All right?"

Angela's eyes looked watery and pale. Brook thought she saw her friend's chin wobble.

"Are you upset?" she asked. "I don't mean to—"

"No!" Angela tossed her hair and gave a little sniff. "I'm not upset." She began to march off, down the sunny hallway.

"So I'll see you after school?" Brook called. "Maybe we can go sledding. Or make a big snow sculpture in the woods?"

"Whatever," Angela replied.

Brook could tell she was hurt.

Great. I can't keep any of my friends happy! she thought, feeling miserable.

But she couldn't worry about that now.

Angela's "help" had landed Brook in deep trouble with the principal. She wasn't sure how she was going to get out of this jam. But shy, A student Brook Lauer was about to face the principal of Whiterock Elementary School . . .

Alone!

★ ★ ★

Everyone was terrified of Mr. Simmons.

He was a tall, serious man, with a mean streak and three rottweilers. Or, at least, that was how the story went. When Brook was in second grade some of the older kids had told her that he kept those attack dogs in his office, just to keep kids in line.

That wasn't true, of course. But he was still a scary guy. When he yelled, the glass rattled in the windows. This principal was not to be messed with.

As Brook turned the corner to his office, her heart did a somersault into her stomach. He was waiting for her! Ms. Yellowfeather had obviously called to let him know she was coming.

Mr. Simmons crossed his arms and looked at her. His shoulders seemed to take up the entire door frame. The man had to be eight feet tall!

Brook swallowed hard.

I sure hope those dogs are well fed. She eased herself into the stiff-backed chair across from Mr. Simmons's desk and folded her hands.

He shook his head slowly, letting out a sad breath. "I'm very, very disappointed in you, Brook.

You've always been such a good student. Such a polite girl. What went wrong?"

"I don't know," she mumbled. For once she wasn't at a loss for words. She could think of a zillion things to say, like: *I got sick of being invisible. So I made a deal with a ghost.* She's *the one who's been misbehaving in class!*

Unfortunately, Mr. Simmons wasn't going to buy a story like that.

Soon he was droning on, lecturing about behaving in class and respecting the teachers. Brook hoped he didn't notice her mind was wandering.

"Do you understand what I'm saying, Ms. Lauer?"

She didn't answer. But she managed a nod.

"Good. You may return to your class. I'm not going to punish you this time," he said. He wrote a brief note for Ms. Yellowfeather. "But if this happens again, your parents will hear about it."

🦇 🦇 🦇

When the final bell rang, Brook rushed to her locker and yanked on her coat. She didn't want to talk to anyone. It was bad enough that she was the class criminal. The last thing she needed was for someone to rub salt in the wound.

She wove through the crowded hallway. She flew down the stairs. She made it to the edge of the lawn when two figures leaped out from behind the hedges.

"Not so fast," Darcy said.

Darcy and Nora stood before her, their faces tight with anger. She was ambushed.

"What's the big idea?" asked Nora. "Trying to give us the slip? We have some talking to do."

"What's happened to you, Brook?" Darcy said, her voice cracking with pain. "Why are you being so mean to us?"

"Talking through the movie, and then blaming me?" Nora shook her head. "That was really finky, you know? Totally and completely finkadelic."

"You really hurt us," Darcy said.

"But I convinced Darcy that there had to be a reason," said Nora. "We're giving you a chance to explain."

"Explain?" Brook croaked. She didn't know what to say! She couldn't tell them the truth, and she never was good at making up lies. Even when it meant protecting someone's feelings.

"So?" Nora prodded.

Brook stared at the frozen ground. "I have nothing to say."

"Nothing?" Darcy croaked. "Tell us why you've been acting so weird! This just isn't like you. You're not yourself!"

Because you wouldn't let me be myself! Brook wanted to shout. *Because you guys always cut me off and boxed me in!*

Tears stung her eyes as she looked up at her friends. "How do you know it's not me? Maybe I've changed. *Maybe I'm not quiet little Brook anymore!*"

Francie's green eyes were thoughtful as she listened. "She actually said that? 'I'm not quiet little Brook anymore?'"

"That's right," Darcy said with a sigh. "And then she just stomped away from us."

Darcy couldn't wait to spill the story of Brook's outburst to Francie and Sam. It was gnawing away at her.

The three kids were out riding horses, their breath puffing out in front of them. The sky was crystal clear. The valley was spread out all around them, rimmed by the Bitterroot Mountains.

Francie was always great for advice. She was only a year older—in *people years*.

But before she became a girl, she had spent hundreds of years as a fairy. Darcy and Sam had met her in Monsterville. Francie had been their unofficial guide during their first trip through the town of monsters and ghouls. When a magic spell had turned her into a real girl, Francie had come home with them for good. Darcy already thought of her as an older sister.

And Sam was in eighth grade. Plus, he came from the big city—Chicago. Smart and wise, he'd helped Darcy through scrapes before.

And at the moment, Darcy needed all the help she could get.

"She was a totally different person," Darcy went on. "A mean, spiteful Brook. She went behind my back to Ms. Yellowfeather. Boy, did I look like an idiot!"

"Pretty strange for Brook," Francie agreed. "She usually doesn't make a peep! I always thought that if I could still work fairy spells, she'd be a great candidate. She's so meek! A little pixie dust would really boost her confidence." She sighed. "Sometimes I miss being a fairy."

"Yeah, I miss you being a fairy, too," Sam snorted. "Especially when I'm holding a flyswatter!"

Francie rolled her eyes. "Watch it, Mackie. You never know, I might still have a trick or two up my sleeve. I could turn your skin plaid!"

"You couldn't turn a *kilt* plaid!" Sam teased.

"You guys!" Darcy broke in. "We were talking about Brook, remember?"

"Right," Sam said. "So, Darce, what do you think made Brook snap like that?"

"Do you think she got tired of you girls never letting her talk?" Francie suggested.

"What's that supposed to mean?" Darcy tugged on both her reins at once and Gingersnap stopped walking.

Francie and Sam pulled their horses up, too. At

least, Sam tried to pull his horse up. He still wasn't too handy in the saddle.

"Well, no offense, Darcy," Francie explained. "But I've noticed that sometimes, Brook starts to say something and you and Nora finish her sentence. She can't get a word in edgewise."

"Oh, Brook doesn't mind," Darcy said. "It's always been like that. She's shy, so Nora and I do a lot of talking for her. She likes it that way!"

"I don't know about that." Francie shook her head. "Last Sunday, when we were making snow angels, I got the impression that Brook was feeling stifled by you guys."

"Francie's got a point," Sam agreed. "Brook might be coming out of her shell. Or at least, trying to."

"People change and grow," Francie said. "But sometimes friends try to keep us on a shelf."

"We'd never do that to Brook," Darcy said, though secretly she sensed the truth in their words.

"I know I've changed a lot since I moved to Whiterock," Sam said. "If you'd told me a year ago that I'd be riding through the woods on the back of one of these overgrown mules instead of riding the El—"

All of a sudden, the horses reared up. Something was spooking them!

Sam clutched his reins as his horse tramped in circles, letting out high-pitched, terrified whinnies.

Darcy pulled Gingersnap's reins in hard, forcing the horse to calm down. She checked the forest around them. "It's just a bird," she announced, squinting at the small creature flying in circles around them. "No, wait. It's a *bat!*"

"Not just any bat!" Francie cheered. "It's Draku!"

In a flash, the bat stretched into a tall, thin vampire. He immediately drew in his black cape and stepped into a shadow.

"Arrgh!" he growled. "I hate coming out here in the daytime. How do you little monsters stand it?" He plunked on a pair of sunglasses and sighed.

"We like the sunshine," Francie teased. "You should try it sometime. Maybe get some color in that pasty white skin of yours."

"Fat chance!" Draku scowled. "Sunshine! Humans are so perverse!"

"What's the matter, Draku?" Darcy piped up. "You're usually cranky. But you seem extra grouchy today."

"Yeah," Sam added. "And what are you doing out of your coffin in the daytime?"

"I hate the day shift," Draku muttered. "But there's trouble in Monsterville. One of those little brats from the Poltergeist Academy has run away. The Grim Reaper sent us to search for her."

"Who's 'us'?" Sam wanted to know. "I only see one of you."

"Draku? Where are you?" A quavery voice floated through the trees.

Darcy hunkered down on her horse. Even though she knew it was someone from Monsterville, the ghostly moan sent a shiver up her spine.

"Over here!" Draku shouted. "You old bat," he added, under his breath.

An old, pinched-looking woman drifted out of the trees and seized Draku by the tip of his pointy ear.

"I heard that, young man," she said in a stern voice. "Don't forget your manners, or I'll ask G. R. to send you to the Academy for a refresher course in monster manners!"

"Unhand me!" Draku whined. The old woman let go of him, and he rubbed at his ear sheepishly. "Miss Prim, this is Darcy Ryan and Sam Mackie. The children who helped save Monsterville."

"I've met Darcy," Miss Prim said, her ancient face lighting up in a kind smile. "I do appreciate your help during our recent troubles!"

"No problem," Sam answered, rubbing his own ear uneasily.

"And I think you know Francie," Draku added. "Former fairy bug."

"Howdy, Miss P.," Francie said with a little wave.

"Francie, Francie, Francie." Miss Prim wagged a finger. "I hope you're better behaved among these humans than you were back in Monsterville!"

"Don't worry. I'm being a good kid." Francie hopped off her horse and grinned. "Usually."

"I never could get Francie to sign up for classes at the Academy," Miss Prim said regretfully.

"Nothing personal, Miss P.," Francie said. "Londontown was just too depressing for this little fairy."

"So what's this about a missing poltergeist?" Darcy wanted to know.

"One of our little ghosts slipped through the cracks," Miss Prim said. "We were taking a field trip. I like to show the children that there's nothing to fear from humans, as long as they keep their distance. So once a year, I bring them up to one of the hills here and we look down on Whiterock."

"You know, blah blah blah . . . Humans are people, too," Draku added wearily. "All that nonsense."

Miss Prim sighed. "It does help them to be better ghosts," she insisted. "Anyway, our little Angela has an attention problem. She seems to think that her intelligence means that she doesn't need to do her schoolwork, and her grades have been slipping lately."

"I can't believe it. Even ghost kids have to go to school?" Sam asked.

"Not just school," Francie laughed. "We're talking the *Academy*. Miss Prim is one tough schoolmarm. She's had centuries of practice!"

"That's right," Miss Prim agreed with a modest smile. "As a result, the Academy produces top-notch ghosts."

"But back to the matter at hand, Miss Prim," Draku said impatiently, pulling his cape tightly around him.

"Yes. Well, Angela was very unhappy at our school. She simply didn't understand what our program had to offer her. I suppose that's why she ran away three days ago."

"So you haven't seen her since Sunday?" Sam asked.

"Well, there *was* that little prank she pulled on Monday," Miss Prim admitted. "I didn't actually see her, but she was clearly involved."

"Don't remind me!" Draku clutched his head with two hands and leaned against a tree. "Every child in that school let out such a caterwauling, my brain is still rattling. What a horrible noise!"

"It's true." Miss Prim shook her head. "She returned to Monsterville on Monday with a human girl. Together, they caused all sorts of problems. The two of them disrupted the entire student body."

"A human girl?" Darcy gasped. "Who would that be? Nobody knows about Monsterville but me, Sam, and Francie."

"And Fiona!" Sam added, thinking of his little sister. "She's always dying to go back to Monsterville. I'll bet it was her!"

"What did she look like?" Francie asked.

"Oh, a regular human girl," Miss Prim said. "About your age, blue eyes, freckles. She had a striking head of hair. It was very long, and carrot red. And she had pulled it back in a ponytail."

Darcy, Francie, and Sam stared at one another. There was no doubt who that could be. It wasn't Fiona.

Red hair, freckles, blue eyes . . .

That was Brook!

No wonder she had been acting so weird.

Their friend was hanging out with a poltergeist!

15

"Miss P., that girl's a friend of ours!" Francie exclaimed.

"It's Brook . . . Brook Lauer," Darcy added. "Angela must have brought her to Monsterville." Darcy's mind raced back to Sunday, when they'd been in the woods. "Wait a second! Brook said she had a new friend. "I'll bet she was talking about Angela."

Quickly, they updated Miss Prim and Draku. "Brook's been acting pretty bizarre lately," Darcy explained. "Maybe Angela's been rubbing off on her."

"Well, this is marvelous!" Miss Prim said. "Draku, we must go pick her up immediately!"

"No way!" Draku scowled. "I've had enough for one day. I'm going to crawl into my coffin and sleep!"

"But, Draku!" Miss Prim cried. "Angela must be brought back as soon as possible."

"First off, we don't know where she is," Draku intoned. "And second, there's the meeting with her parents."

Miss Prim let out a horrified gasp. "Oh, her parents! They're supposed to arrive tonight!"

"Great," Sam muttered. "A ghost reunion."

"Angela's parents sent a message," Miss Prim explained. "They aren't able to haunt their restaurant anymore. So they're coming to Monsterville. I have to be there to greet them . . . and report on Angela."

Draku pulled his cape up to his nose and glared at Miss Prim. "If we start chasing around Whiterock now, we'll never get back in time for the meeting."

"We'll find Angela for you," Francie said.

"That would be very helpful," Miss Prim said.

"It's settled then," Draku confirmed. "Coffin, here I come."

"But do be careful," Miss Prim warned the kids. "Angela has plenty of tricks up her sleeve." With a final smile, the woman floated off.

"Finally," Draku grumbled. "Adiós." With that, he twisted himself into a tall licorice stick. Then the black stick shrank into a bat again. He flitted around Miss Prim's head as they headed into the woods.

"See ya later, Draku!" Sam called out. "Don't let the bedbugs bite!"

A screech wafted back through the air.

Sam turned back to Darcy and Francie. "Well? What's your plan?" he asked.

"No plan," Francie admitted. "Miss Prim seemed so worried, I had to offer. But how are we going to get Angela back to Monsterville?"

"And away from Brook!" Darcy looked stricken. "I can't believe I got so mad at her. I should have known why she was acting so obnoxious!"

"It does make sense," Francie agreed. "Angela must have been coaching her."

"I feel like a jerk. I've got to apologize," Darcy said, swinging back into Gingersnap's saddle.

"And we've got to find out if she knows where Angela is," Francie said, hopping onto her own horse.

"Hang on, you guys," Sam called. He stuffed one foot into a stirrup and hoisted himself into the saddle.

"Would you hurry up, Sam?" Francie called back.

"We need your advice," Darcy added. "We've got to figure out a way to save Brook."

Sam prodded his horse and sighed. "Time for a wild ghost chase."

🦇 🦇 🦇

If finding a ghost was difficult, finding Brook was impossible.

No one was home at the Lauer house. She wasn't on the school grounds. Or at the Dairy Saloon. Sam went through the stacks at the library, while Darcy and Francie peeked into the Short Cuts hair salon. No sign of Brook.

Finally, they spotted Mrs. Lauer outside the grocery store. She was loading groceries into the back of a Jeep. "I thought she was with you," Brook's mother said with concern. She left the house with her sled nearly an hour ago."

"Thanks, Mrs. Lauer," Darcy said, backing away. She turned to Francie and Sam, and they all said it at the same time:

"Winslow Hill!"

Sam had to rush home to tutor a friend. Total brains like Sam didn't go untapped! The girls said good-bye and made a beeline for the hill.

Winslow Hill was the sledding center of Whiterock. It was huge, steep, and more fun than a roller coaster! Most kids went sledding on the side facing the town.

On the other side was the Challenge: a steeper hill that was also an obstacle course. There were three trees that the sledder had to steer around. One false move, and you'd either be flattened against one of them, or dumped into a deep, watery ditch. The Challenge was for expert sledders only.

But Brook wasn't going down either side of Winslow Hill. She was perched forlornly on her sled, knocking her boots together. When she saw the girls, she turned away and started rolling snow into a ball.

"Brook, please. Will you just listen to us?" Darcy begged.

"We only want to help," Francie added.

"I don't feel like talking to you guys," Brook said. "How did you find me, anyway?"

"We turned Whiterock upside down." Darcy poked Brook's toboggan with her toe. "And if you ask me, sledding by yourself is a pretty weird activity."

Brook sighed. "I wanted to be away from everyone," she admitted, packing the snow in her hands. She looked up at Darcy. "Why are you talking to me, anyway? Aren't you mad about the way I've been acting?"

"That's just it," Darcy said, sitting down next to Brook on the toboggan. "I don't think *you* were the one doing that. Were you?"

Francie knelt in front of Brook. "That was Angela, wasn't it?"

Brook jumped up as if they had given her an electrical shock. "What—! How do you know about Angela?" she demanded.

"We know about all of it," Darcy went on. "Angela. Monsterville. The whole thing."

"Monsterville?" Brook narrowed her eyes. "Angela called it Mustardville."

Suddenly, the puzzle pieces began to fit together. Of course! Where else would a ghost live but in a town called Monsterville! And that weird man—the vampire! He belonged there, too.

"Brook, we've been there, too," Darcy said, breaking into her thoughts. "It's a really cool place. But I'm afraid Angela isn't as good a friend as you think she is."

Brook set her jaw. "Oh, really? She's been a better friend than you are! She likes me a lot. She listens when I talk. And she thinks I'm funny!"

"I think you're funny, too!" Darcy insisted.

"No, you don't! I'm just somebody who'll hold your horse while you make snow angels."

Darcy sighed. "I deserved that," she said. "But you've got to admit, Angela has caused you a lot of trouble. And if she's such a great pal, where is she right now?"

Brook's face fell. "I don't exactly know," she

admitted. "We had a fight. But I'm sure she's not—"

"Yo, Dudettes!" a cheerful voice greeted them.

The girls looked over to see Nora trudging up the hill, her sled trailing behind her.

Darcy put a finger to her lips. "We can talk about this later," she said. "Nora doesn't know about you-know-who."

"I thought I saw you going past my house, so I grabbed my sled and caught up with you," Nora explained breathlessly. "Oh my gosh! Wait till I tell you guys what happened! It was so funny! I had to go to the doctor's office, right? And I was in the waiting room. And I hear someone inside yelling at the doctor. . . ."

Nora chattered away happily. She didn't seem to notice the tension among the other girls. And if she was still mad about what Brook had done in school that day, she didn't show it. Nora wasn't one to hold a grudge.

Good old Nora and her endless stories, thought Darcy.

"Hey! I'm getting cold just sitting here," Nora said. "Let's do some sledding before it gets dark!"

"I'm game," Francie agreed. "Can you steer that thing?" she asked, eyeing Nora's rusty sled.

"Oh, sure," Nora assured her. "This rope is tied to the front part, so I just have to give it a good yank, and it'll turn."

"Nora's an expert sledder," Darcy explained.

Nora hopped on the sled. The red runners sank

into the snow as she pulled herself up to the edge of the hill.

"Check me out, guys," Nora said with a whoop. "I'm going to take the Challenge!"

"Should she be doing that?" Francie asked.

"She's a pro," Darcy assured her.

"Here goes!" Nora said, shooting down the hill.

"All right, Nora!" Brook cheered, forgetting her sulk for a second.

The sled zigzagged past a fat tree, then swerved onto the fast track.

"Nice move!" Darcy shouted.

But halfway down the hill, out of nowhere, the figure of a girl shot up out of the snow. Her arms stretched out before her, grabbing at Nora. A ghostly, ear-piercing shriek cut through the air.

Darcy's blood turned to ice when she saw the face of the ghost girl, contorted and gloomy. Her lips were a slash. Her eyes were an eerie mesmerizing blue. . . .

Time seemed to stand still. Darcy knew that it was just Angela, but Nora panicked. She threw her arms over her face in a terrified gesture. Nora's sled veered wildly out of control.

"Steer!" Brook shouted.

"Nora! Open your eyes and—"

But it was too late.

As the girls watched in horror, Nora's sled skidded off the path and slid toward the ditch!

16

"Nora!"

The girls rushed down into the ditch, sliding through the snow to reach their friend.

Nora's sled lay on its side. A few feet away, a shaken Nora sat waist-deep in cold water. She had broken through the ice.

Her face was ashen and her eyes were glazed.

"Are you all right?" Darcy asked.

Nora shook her head slightly. "I think I'm okay," she said weakly. She was shaking violently. And when she tried to stand up, her knees buckled under her.

Darcy and Brook grabbed her arms and helped her up the embankment.

"I thought I saw—," Nora said. Then she stopped. "Did you see—?" But a sob cut her short. "I'm so cold," she wailed. "And I think I saw a ghost!"

"There was some kind of trick of the light," Francie said comfortingly. "A weird reflection from the sunset. I saw it. Didn't you guys?"

"Oh, yeah, that was really weird," Darcy said. "And did you hear that wind howling?" She switched subjects quickly. She didn't want Nora to know the truth . . .

That she *had* seen a real, live ghost.

"We've got to get you home, Nora," Brook insisted. "You'll catch cold in these wet clothes!"

Nora just nodded. She looked so feeble! Darcy and Francie supported her as she stumbled up the steep hill. Behind them, Brook picked up her bent-up sled.

"Good thing we're not too far from Nora's house," Darcy said. "Right, Brook?"

But Brook just dragged the sled along, sober and silent. This was all her fault!

🦇 🦇 🦇

"Thank you again, girls. If you hadn't been there when Nora went through that ice . . ." Mrs. Chambers glanced anxiously upstairs, where the doctor was examining Nora. "Anyway, everything's all right now."

"We'll check in on Nora tomorrow," Darcy said. "After school."

"I'm sure she'll be shipshape by then. Dr. Hellerstein says she's just shaken up." Nora's mom smiled reassuringly. "Bye, girls."

"Bye!" Darcy and Francie called out.

Brook waved, but she didn't say anything. She hadn't said much at all since Nora's accident.

Guilt ate away at her as they headed back to Winslow Hill to pick up Brook's toboggan. It was her fault that Angela was here in Whiterock. It was her fault that Nora went into the ice. It could have been so much worse!

The mountains that lined the valley rose around them, and the sun was just setting. In the dark blue twilight, Brook let out a deep sigh. She couldn't stand this horrible feeling!

By the time they reached the top of the hill, Brook was worn down. "All right, all right," she said. "I admit it. You were right. Angela means well. But she's also a lot of trouble." She kicked at her toboggan.

Their footsteps crunched to a halt. Darcy and Francie faced her.

"Tell us where she's staying," Darcy said.

"We have to get her back home, where she belongs," Francie added.

"I don't know where she is," Brook admitted. "We got into an argument. I wanted her to stop meddling with my life. She got mad and took off."

"You mean she disappeared?" Francie asked.

Brook nodded. "And even if we found her, she wouldn't listen to me." She kicked at the snow and turned away. Dragging her toboggan, she headed home.

Francie and Darcy followed.

"Whether she's mad at you or not, you're probably the only person she'll listen to," Francie pointed out.

"But I don't know what to do!" Brook wailed. "This is all so messed up. I don't know how to fix it!"

"That's why you've got buds like us," Darcy

said. "Don't freak out. I'll think of something!"

Then she stopped herself. "I mean . . . we'll come up with a plan, together. As long as you trust us. That's the important part."

Brook gave a weak smile. "Oh, I trust you. The fact is, Angela drives me a little crazy." She looked down at the ground. "I'm glad you're not still mad at me. I've been acting kind of poopy lately."

"Wellll . . ." Darcy slung an arm around her friend's shoulder. "I've been kind of poopy, too."

"I'm sorry, too," Francie added. "I should have realized that you were feeling left out at the sleep-over."

"Well, I should have said something, instead of just feeling sorry for—wait a minute!" Brook stopped short. "Hang on a second. I didn't think of it before, but how did you guys find out about Monsterville? And Angela? And how come you weren't scared when she popped out of the hill like that?"

"Now, that's a long story," Darcy said. "I'll tell you all the gory details sometime. Let's just say I've made some ghoulish friends lately. And I've been to Monsterville a couple of times."

"That's really the name of the little town?" Brook was bursting with excitement. "Does that mean what it sounds like? Is it really a whole *town* full of monsters?"

"It's the only place they could find where they could all live together safely," Darcy explained.

Francie nodded. "When Angela took you there, you were right smack in the middle of the biggest collection of ghouls, goblins, and creepy creatures in the world!"

Brook's head was spinning. Monsterville? Creepy creatures? And she thought a houseful of ghosts would be scary!

She turned to Francie. "What about you?" she asked. "How come you know about this place?"

Francie flashed her a mischievous smile. "Where do you think I came from?"

"You're from Monsterville?" Brook was floored. "Are you a ghost, too?"

"She's a fairy," Darcy piped up.

"Ex-fairy," Francie stressed. "Darcy helped me get a one-way ticket to being human. No fairy dust left."

"Wowsie." Brook gasped. "This is totally crazy. I had no idea!" Now it started to make sense: Francie's sudden appearance on the scene. Her tiny, pixie-like frame. And Darcy's special attachment to her.

By this time, they had reached the Lauers' gray cedar house. Brook could see her parents inside, getting dinner ready. The cozy rooms were all lit up, and the house looked warm and inviting.

But Brook couldn't forget that danger was lurking in Whiterock. "Where do you think Angela will strike next?" she whispered.

"Don't worry," Francie reassured her. "From what Miss Prim said, Angela's not vicious. She's just got a stubborn streak. We'll figure out a way to coax her home."

"I'm really sorry," Brook added. "About everything."

"Would you quit apologizing?" Darcy said, giving her a quick squeeze. "It's our fault for trouncing on you. If we'd let you be yourself, you wouldn't have needed a ghost to speak up for you."

"For now," added Francie, "let's just worry about getting out of this jam together!"

"Okay." Brook gave her friends a final wave and went into the house. Her heart lifted as she took off her snow gear and her boots. She slipped her feet into warm slippers and thought about Darcy and Francie.

It felt great, knowing she had her friends in her corner!

As she went upstairs to her room, all Brook wanted to do was land in her bed like a meteorite and fall asleep. It had been a totally exhausting day.

She sat in front of her vanity. Dots of pink lit the center of her cheeks. But her hair was like a wiry orange mop. She picked up a brush . . .

And felt that icy wind on her neck.

"Angela?" she asked, swiveling around. There was no one in the room with her. She turned back to the mirror again.

And let out a sharp gasp.

Lurking over her shoulders was the reflection of a pale-faced, puffed-up ghost!

Brook put a hand over her heart. It was beating like a drumroll. The spunky ghost had startled her.

Angela collapsed on the floor, laughing hysterically. "Oh, that was so great!" she gasped, finally catching her breath.

"I'm glad you thought it was funny," Brook muttered.

"I'm just so good at haunting!" Angela said. "You know all about me, and I still scared you!"

"A real laugh riot," Brook said sarcastically. "And that other stuff wasn't funny, either."

Angela sat up, looking hurt. "What other stuff?" she asked innocently.

"You know. The stuff at school today. That was downright mean! And getting Nora in that accident. She could have been seriously hurt!"

"Oh, *pull-lease*." Angela flopped backward on the bed. "A little tumble never hurt anyone! That's what did me in." She sat up and flopped her head onto her shoulders again, showing how her neck was broken. She rolled her eyes back in their sockets and her skin turned blue. *"Bleeeah!"*

"Ugh! Gross." Brook was totally exasperated. "Listen, Angela. It's time for you to head home."

"Back to the Academy?" Angela sniffed. "Ha! That's no home!"

"It's home if there's someone there who cares about you," Brook insisted. "They're looking for you, Angela. They're worried and—"

"Bo-ring." Angela sniffed, returning her head to its normal state. She squinted and ribbons of a gross liquid started drizzling down the walls.

"What are you doing?" Brook asked. "Excuse me, I'm trying to talk to you!"

The icky goop kept dripping.

Brook threw her hands up in the air. "You are so immature."

Eyes blazing, Angela jumped up. The goo dried up and disappeared, but Brook barely noticed. "Immature?" the ghost snapped. "I'm more than a hundred and twenty-five years old."

Brook rolled her eyes. "It doesn't matter how old you are if you act like a total jerk! You're so interested in having a good time, you don't care who gets in trouble."

"You little wimp!" Angela's lips formed a grim line. "I was helping you. But you just want to stay in your shell and let your friends walk all over you."

"That's not true." Brook fought back the tears that stung her eyes. "I want to be my own person. You're the one who's been walking all over me!"

"I was just trying to help," Angela insisted.

"I appreciate it. But I'd like to try taking care of myself. Without *anyone's* help."

"Fine." Angela stood up. "Well, I can haunt without *your* help. I don't need you to turn this town upside down. I can do it all by myself!"

"No . . . wait!" Brook shouted.

But it was too late. Angela's body faded into a thin film. All Brook could see was her glowing blue eyes. The eyes blazed for a second, then the sheer ghost laughed and floated out through the wall.

Brook went to the window. Outside, lights from other houses glimmered like jewels.

Most of the people in Whiterock were making dinner. Kids were doing their homework. Parents were reading the newspaper.

They didn't know there was an angry renegade ghost out there.

And Brook was the one who had made her mad.

At school the next day, Brook felt self-conscious. As soon as she walked into the room, she could tell that kids were talking about her. She heard whispers as she sat at her desk.

There was no denying it. With those stupid jokes during the frog movie, she'd made a total idiot of herself.

She could only hope that Angela wouldn't make a return appearance today.

"Hey, Brook," Jay whispered. "Are you going to get kicked out of class again today?"

Darcy shot him a warning look. But Brook knew she was going to have to clean up her own mess. If she didn't want her friends to overshadow her, she had to stand up for herself.

"I don't think so," Brook whispered back. She grinned at Jay. "That wasn't really me yesterday."

"Who was it, your evil twin?"

A few kids in the class tittered. Ms. Yellowfeather looked up.

"Brook was talking to Jay," Annabel Mackinac announced. She tossed her curls and flashed the teacher a sickly sweet smile.

The teacher frowned. "I can see that, Annabel. Does anyone know where Nora Chambers is today?"

"She's staying home," Darcy informed her. "She spun out on her sled yesterday. The doctor said she should take it easy."

"Oh! I hope she's all right," Ms. Yellowfeather said in a concerned voice.

I hope so, too, Brook said silently.

The teacher finished taking attendance and stood up. "In light of yesterday's mishaps, I thought a new attendance monitor would be in order. Annabel, would you like to take this to the office?"

"Would I!" Annabel strutted up for the prize.

Darcy turned around and mimicked her *Aren't I wonderful?* face for Brook.

Although Brook had lost the job for good, she and Darcy were friends again. And when Nora got back to school, they'd all be buddies. And that was what really mattered.

By the time the final bell rang, Brook sighed in relief. She'd made it through the day on her own with no help—or trouble—from Angela.

That was the good news.

The bad news was, there was no sign of the ghost girl. How were they going to get her back to Monsterville if they couldn't find her?

"Maybe she's gone for good," Darcy said hopefully. The girls were standing on the school lawn, where they'd met up with Francie.

"It sounds like you were really firm with Angela last night," Darcy added. "Maybe she finally got the message."

"Don't count on it," Brook warned. "She hates that Academy. She'd never go back on her own."

The three girls walked up a side street, toward the Dairy Saloon on Main Street.

Darcy shuddered. "It gives me the creeps knowing she's out there." She lowered her voice. "She could be listening in on us now!"

Brook nodded. "And if I know Angela, she's got something up her sleeve."

"Maybe she—" Francie blinked. "What's that?"

"Thunder?" Brook listened to the distant rumbling. "But the sky is clear."

"It's a storm." Francie pointed east.

In the wide, bright sky was a small, dark cluster of clouds. Churning and twisting, the clouds formed a funnel shape. Below the vortex, the wind was so furious it sucked up snow and branches like a vacuum.

"It's a tornado," Darcy shouted over the howling wind. "We've got to get shelter—*now!*"

Rushing onto Main Street, the girls ran to the nearest building—the General Store. They yanked open the doors to the storm cellar and clambered in.

"Hurry!" Brook shouted, choking on dust.

Francie hopped in behind her. Together they reached up and slammed the doors shut.

The old cellar was dark and musty. The only light came from a small window overlooking the street. Francie rushed over and peered out.

"Stay away from the window!" Brook shouted. "The storm could shatter the glass."

The three girls huddled on some wooden crates. Overhead, wind shrieked and ice pelted the ground.

"This is weird," Darcy muttered. "We never have tornadoes in the dead of winter."

Just then, the wind howled a lonesome whine. Brook shivered, sure that the wind was calling her name. Was she losing her mind?

But then it happened again . . . *"Broooook!"*

"Did you hear that?" Francie asked.

Suddenly, a burst of light shot through the dark cellar. Just outside the window, a pair of blue sparks flashed furiously.

Brook gasped, recognizing the blue dots of light.

Angela's eyes!

"Did you see that?" Darcy asked. "Is it a fire?"

"More like a fiery temper," Francie said, folding her arms.

"I recognize those eyes," Brook said. She pointed toward the window. "That's no ordinary tornado out there. It's Angela."

"The little twerp," Francie muttered. "Doesn't she understand that storms can cause major damage?"

Darcy cringed as something banged against the cellar doors. "This Angela is the worst monster I've ever met," Darcy said, flipping her braids over her shoulders.

"She's just a kid," Francie reminded her.

"Exactly," Darcy said. "Which makes her totally unpredictable!"

After the storm passed, the girls pushed their way out of the cellar. Brook was afraid of what she might see, but Whiterock seemed to have fared okay.

Mr. Ellison's truck was stopped at an odd angle, and Main Street was covered in snowdrifts. People were stepping out of the buildings and assessing the damage.

The girls were outside Paws 'n' Claws when Sheriff Smoke's red pickup truck pulled up. He hopped out and slammed the door behind him.

"Everybody okay? Is anyone hurt?" he asked.

"Everything's fine, Sheriff," Mr. Putnam said, stepping out of the General Store. "I thought I heard the doors to my cellar banging, though."

Darcy piped up. "That was us. We hid in the storm cellar."

"Good thinking, kids," Sheriff Smoke said. He shook his head. "I've never seen a storm kick up so fast and furious."

"Sure made a mess," Mr. Putnam said. "We're going to have to get this place cleaned up."

Cleaned up? The words echoed in Brook's head. Angela would hate that.

As the two men turned away, the girls looked at one another.

"That brat!" Darcy was seething. "Angela may be from the spirit realm, but she's totally obnoxious!"

"You know what?" Brook said.

"But she's just a kid," Francie insisted. "And when I lived in Monsterville, I always thought the little poltergeists were so cute. They used to—"

"Hey, you guys," Brook interrupted.

"Gingersnap must be scared stiff," Darcy babbled. "What if that storm hit the ranch and—"

"Excuse me! You guys!" Brook shouted.

Darcy and Francie blinked in surprise.

"Wow! I got your attention," Brook said, grinning. "Something Mr. Putnam said just jogged my brain."

"And . . . ?" Francie prodded.

Brook rubbed her mittened hands together. "I think I know how to get Angela back to Monsterville."

🦇 🦇 🦇

A few hours later, dusk was settling across Whiterock. Most of the adults were out rounding up horses and kids, and collecting things that had scattered in the storm.

In the dusty, dank attic of her house, Brook sat alone, trying to make contact with Angela.

Ugh. This attic was the creepiest place on earth. Old stuff was packed in boxes and piled against the walls. Gray cobwebs clung to the beams, and there was a thin layer of dust and lint over everything.

Brook had always hated it up here, even in broad daylight. In the fading, dim light of sunset, it was much spookier.

A few big pieces of furniture, like the cedar chest and a walnut wardrobe, were covered with white sheets. Brook knew they were harmless. Still, she kept imagining creepy things lurking under the strange shapes.

Some old photographs of unidentified relatives glared at her. Maybe they were wondering why they were stuck up here in the attic. Maybe they were angry about it.

Brook shuddered. *What am I doing up here?* she wondered. *I don't even know if this is going to work.* Still, it was the only chance she had.

She ran her hands through the dust, swirling it up a little. Then she reached behind a cardboard box and swept out some dust bunnies.

"At-*choo!*" She let out a little sneeze, feeling miserable. She was filthy. She was alone in the attic. It was dark. So where was Angela?

She was about to sneeze again when she felt that icy wind blow through the attic. She held her breath as one of the old pictures glared at her with angry blue eyes.

Then the picture winked.

Angela stepped out of it and walked through the shadows of the attic, toward Brook.

"Why so bummy, dummy?" she asked, looking amused. "You seemed pretty anxious to get rid of me yesterday. Then I come back to check on you and here you are, covered with soot."

"Angela, you were right," Brook said, hoping her acting skills were up to par. "I'm sorry. I should have listened to you."

"Oh, really?" Angela inspected her fingernails. "Tell me all about it."

"My friends were horrible," Brook lied. "They can't take a little joke!"

Angela smiled smugly. Brook thought she was being a little melodramatic . . . but Angela seemed to buy the whole act.

"On top of everything else," Brook went on, "I realized that I can't do anything without you. I'm a complete weenie without you! Will you come back?"

Angela crossed her arms and rolled her eyes. "Ooohh, I don't know," she said doubtfully.

"Please?" Brook begged.

"You said some pretty harsh stuff last night," Angela pointed out.

You weren't exactly Miss Sensitivity! Brook thought. But she kept her mouth clamped shut. She had to get Angela to agree to her plan.

"What did you think of my tornado?" Angela asked, her eyes bright with pride.

"Awesome!" Brook congratulated her. "It was the best thing I ever saw. Really scary!"

"Gee, thanks," Angela beamed. Brook could see she was doing a good job of buttering her up.

"Angela, you've just got to be my friend again. I'll do anything to make up with you!" Brook snapped her fingers, as if she had just thought of a plan. "I know! I'll go back to Monsterville with you. This time, we can really scare the kids at the Academy!"

Intrigued, Angela crossed her arms. "Do you have a new idea?"

"The best ever," Brook said. "So good, it can't wait." She pushed the trapdoor open and stepped down. "I'll tell you about it on the way."

She studied the ghost hopefully. Would Angela go for it? Would she take the bait?

Angela hesitated a second, then grinned. She floated down through the rafters. "Let's do it!"

"But Brook, how are we going to convince the kids that you're a ghost buster?" Angela asked.

The two girls were hurrying through the dark woods, headed toward Monsterville.

"That's why I have this bag," Brook explained. She was lugging a heavy canvas duffel behind her. "There's a secret weapon inside. Any human kid would know it's just one of those strap-on five-gallon water pistols. But poltergeists will think it's some kind of ghost-catching equipment!"

"This is gonna be great!" Angela flitted back and forth, trying to prod Brook forward.

"Plus I've got a disguise. A jumpsuit and a helmet with a mask," Brook went on, huffing and puffing. "They won't recognize me from Monday. With my hair up and my face covered, I'll look like a member of the ghost patrol!"

"Nice going, Brooksie. But step it up," Angela said impatiently.

"I can't help it," Brook said breathlessly. She dropped the bag and sat down on it, fanning herself. "This stuff is so heavy. I forgot I was going to have to travel so far!"

"Just leave it. The kids at the Academy will be getting ready for bed soon!"

"Angela! I can't go ghost busting without his stuff."

"Aargh!" Angela moaned. "At this rate we're never going to get there."

Brook looked up at her forlornly. "I wish you could help me."

Angela eyed the straps dubiously. Brook knew there was no way those transparent ghost fingers could lift the bag. She held her breath, hoping Angela would think of the same solution she had in mind.

"Why don't I just hop into you? That way, there'd be two of us lugging it along," Angela suggested.

"Oh! Great idea," Brook said brightly. "I should have thought of that myself."

Angela disappeared, and Brook felt herself jump a little as her body was taken over. Angela let out a grunt as she lifted the heavy bag onto her shoulder.

"Ugh! What have you got in here, rocks?"

Not exactly—there are a couple of bricks, though, Brook thought. Then she wiped her mind clean and concentrated on ghost busting.

Angela grew tired much more quickly than usual. Brook could feel it. The heavy bag, plus the climb up the trail to the cave, wore her down.

For the first time, Brook felt like her plan had a chance of working!

They finally got to the crystal tunnel and ran

into Monsterville. This time, Brook looked around a lot more carefully.

So this is Monsterville, she thought.

It was so obvious now! This was no regular little town like Whiterock. It was a hodgepodge of different spooky places—a home for every kind of monster! She wanted to check the town out more closely. But right now she had a job to do.

The first thing she did was turn five cartwheels in a row. Then she started spinning in circles, whirling around as fast as she could.

"Hey—stop—whoa! What are you doing?" Angela objected in a weak voice.

"I'm sorry!" Brook answered. "I'm just so excited about the plan. I can't help myself!"

But it was clear to Brook that her hunch was right. If tasting bubble gum was a major adventure for Angela, then spinning around was a total overload of the senses!

"I have to rest," Angela complained.

"Not yet! Let's climb that tree," Brook suggested.

"No way, I have to lie down." Angela slumped out of Brook's body and collapsed woozily on the ground. "Ugh. How can you stand that tumbling? I feel like I've just been through a washing machine," she moaned.

"Don't you want to terrify the kids at the Academy?" Brook asked.

"I just want to lie here." Angela wasn't just pale—she was distinctly green.

"I thought so. Okay!" Brook called out.

Quick as a flash, figures leaped out of the surrounding woods. Brook recognized Miss Prim and that vampire who'd tried to sniff her out.

But the others . . .

She couldn't help but shudder.

A snarling werewolf with a muzzle full of teeth.

Old, wrinkled witches.

Huge, white bearish creatures with long claws.

Festering zombies.

The monsters were here . . . and they were steaming mad!

The creatures surrounded Angela, forming a circle. A hooded figure stepped forward and pointed a curved hatchet at the young ghost.

"You've caused us all a great deal of worry," he said in a raspy voice. "Time to pay the price." He motioned the schoolteacher ahead. "Miss Prim . . . if you will."

Brook would have been scared out of her wits if it weren't for her friends. Darcy and Francie had emerged from the bushes, too. They each took one hand and squeezed hard, letting her know it was okay.

"Let me outta here!" Angela tried to scramble up, but Miss Prim pressed her back with a thorny finger of ghostly light.

"Don't move a muscle, young lady," the teacher said. "You've caused enough trouble with your escapades for monsters and humans alike."

Angela collapsed again, pinned down by the ghostly light. "All right, you win," she groused. "I'm busted." She turned to glare at Brook, adding, "No thanks to you, chump."

Miss Prim lowered her hand and the ribbon of

light faded. "We're grateful to this young human for bringing you home," she said firmly.

Brook bit her lip. "I just wanted what was best for everyone," she said, watching the monsters cautiously. "Sure, Angela caused some problems. But she also gave me the push I needed. She's a good kid."

"Good for a chase," Miss Prim said, fixing Angela with a stern look. "We have gone to great lengths to find you. You had me worried to distraction!"

"But you don't understand!" Angela complained. "I just wanted to taste things. I wanted to feel things! I haven't been inside a real body for more than a hundred years. I couldn't stand to sit around in that school any longer!"

"My dear," Miss Prim said, "once you have learned to be a ghost, you may haunt all you like. Believe me, you'll get there. But in the meantime, you must stay in school. You have a lot of catching up to do!"

"I do not," Angela mumbled. "I know perfectly well how to be a ghost."

"You know many things that the other students don't know," Miss Prim admitted. "And perhaps your experience could be valuable in the classroom."

"It could?" Angela looked surprised.

"Yes, my dear. In fact, I think all our students should be able to bring some of their—er—practical knowledge into the classroom. How does assisting a teacher in a class or two sound?"

Angela looked down at her clumpy old-fashioned boots. "It wouldn't stink," she admitted. "And maybe I could use some of that stuff you teach the other kids."

"Like learning how to move things?" Brook suggested.

"Don't rub it in," Angela said, glancing over at Brook. "You never would have been able to trick me like that if I could have lifted the bag by myself!"

"I'm sorry I tricked you," Brook said.

"It was a good plan," Angela said, giving Brook a rueful smile. "I gotta give you credit, Brooksie. I didn't know you had it in you!"

"And we had no idea how much trouble you could cause!" a voice said. Angela turned around, looking for the source.

Suddenly, a ghostly couple floated into the circle. The man was wearing overalls, and the woman was wearing a long gingham dress and a white apron. She was holding a toddler, who reached out toward Angela.

Brook realized with a shock that this must be Angela's family.

"Ma? Pa?" Angela rushed over to her parents and threw her arms around them. "It's so good to see you!"

"We've missed you, Angie," the man said, ruffling her hair.

"Angie-wangie," said the tiny ghost. He waddled through the air and gave Angela a hug.

"Leo!" Angela gasped. "You're still just a little squirt."

"And he's got a few ghost lessons to learn, too," said Angela's father.

"I hope you'll be more willing to behave yourself if we're living nearby," the woman said softly. She patted her daughter on the shoulder. "We're all going to be together again. Home to stay."

"Aw. Ma . . ." Angela looked up sheepishly. "You sound just like Brook."

"A very good influence," the ghost woman said. She beamed a smile at Brook. "Even if she *is* human."

🦇 🦇 🦇

"Brook, you were awesome!" Darcy clapped her friend on the back.

The three girls were walking toward the exit from Monsterville.

"Thanks," Brook said, glancing nervously over her shoulder. A parade of monsters was following them.

"I know, it takes a little getting used to," Darcy agreed. "But they really grow on you."

At the cave door, Darcy and Francie turned to say their good-byes to the crowd. Brook counted five witches, two tall, hairy werewolves, a whole family of white yetis, three zombies . . . and a bunch of other funny-looking monsters she couldn't even identify.

"Farewell, Frances," said the hooded figure. Brook didn't know his name, but she got the feeling he was in charge of the monster town.

"Bye, G. R.," Francie said with a bright smile. "Sam will be sorry he missed you."

"I'll bet," the hooded creature rasped.

Brook swallowed hard as they cheerfully waved their arms, paws, and bones in farewell.

"Bye, guys!" Darcy called out. "Don't be strangers!"

"See you later, Creep-a-nators," Francie yelled.

Her throat tight with fear, Brook could only wave. She didn't have the nerve to actually talk to the ghoulish crowd!

With a final wave, the girls turned away and ducked into the crystal tunnel.

"Another monster adventure behind us," Darcy said, sighing. "It's lucky that Brook came up with that—"

"Wait!" Brook interrupted her. "Just hold on one second." She turned and pressed toward the cave opening. She had to do it. If she'd learned anything, it was that she needed to speak up for herself.

Swallowing hard, she darted out into the open air. The monster crowd was just breaking up. "Hey . . . uh, folks," she called, forcing a brave smile.

"Brook?" Miss Prim blinked. "Did you forget something, dear?"

"Just wanted to say . . . thanks for all your help," she said. "I never thought it would take a . . . a *ghost* to scare me out of my shell."

A low sound rumbled through the monster crowd.

Were they mad?

No . . . they were laughing.

They liked her joke!

Brook grinned. "Well . . . good-bye! Happy haunting! And sweet screams!"

The monsters laughed and cheered. Brook's heart swelled with pride. Beaming, she walked back into the cave.

"You know, you were great back there," Francie said as they made their way through the crystal tunnel. "That took a whole lot of nerve—fooling Angela like that, and letting her hop into your body."

"Plus that plan! It worked like a charm," Darcy added.

"Thanks," Brook said. "I just hope I don't get grounded forever. My parents are going to freak if they find out I snuck out of the house."

Darcy slung an arm around her friend. "We'll come up with something."

"Maybe we can say we were doing midnight sledding?" Brook wondered aloud. "Or that we had to go stargazing! That we had to make notes on the constellations for science class."

Darcy grinned. "I guess from now on, we're not going to be able to shut you up, huh?"

"I don't know about that," Brook said. "But you're definitely going to be hearing a lot more from me!"

There's more spooky

adventure coming your way in

Beware the Claw!

by R. A. Noonan

Here's a spine-tingling preview . . .

POP! A cinder burst in the fireplace, making Fiona Mackie jump. "What was that?"

"Just the fire." Eleven-year-old Darcy Ryan pulled her younger cousin closer on the sofa. With the lights out and shadows dancing across the room, no wonder Fiona was spooked. She was only six.

"I thought it was the Claw," Fiona whispered, burrowing her head into the crook of Darcy's arm.

"It could be," Sam Mackie said. "The Claw loves to come out at night in snowstorms. And it's snowing like crazy out there."

Outside the wide, paned window of the Ryans' living room, white flakes drifted through the night. Since it was Friday, their parents had agreed to let Fiona and Sam stay over at the Ryan ranch. It was the perfect night to huddle by a warm fire and play games. But somehow they'd gotten on the subject of the Claw, Montana's most notorious woodland creature.

"D-d-does the Claw ever break into houses?" Fiona asked, her voice quavering.

"He's unstoppable," Sam said, his dark eyes glimmering. Thirteen-year-old Sam was usually pretty serious about things. But sometimes he liked to make his pesky little sister squirm.

"Cut it out, Sam," Francie said. "You're scaring Fee." She stood up and tossed her ginger hair over the shoulder of her cable-knit sweater. "I'm going to make cocoa. Why don't you guys break out Monopoly or Nintendo or something?"

"I want to know more about the Claw," Fiona insisted as Francie disappeared into the kitchen. "What does it look like? Has it ever hurt anyone? Does it ever . . . *eat children*?"

"It's just an old legend," Darcy said. "Some hunter probably saw a bear in the woods and made up a big story about it."

"The Claw is no ordinary bear," Sam insisted. "Hunters say it's an awesome ugly sight. And its right paw is contorted."

"*Cavorted*? What's that mean?" Fiona asked. Her dark eyes were bright with fear.

"*Contorted*. It's sort of . . . twisted," Sam said in an eerie voice. Shadows made his eyes look like two black holes. "The paw is huge, with talons that are six inches long. Six inches!"

"Oooh!" Fiona hugged Darcy tight.

Darcy patted her cousin's shoulder and tried to imagine it. Six-inch nails weren't very practical in the woods. And she'd lived her whole life in this wooded section of the Bitterroot Mountains. Darcy had always thought the Claw legend was sort of silly, but Sam made it sound real. His rasping voice sent a little chill up her spine.

"That giant paw is how the beast got its name," Sam continued. "That, and the fact that it growls at everyone it meets. It clenches its deadly teeth and snarls, *'Beware the Claw! Beware the Claw!'*"

Shadows danced over the silent room. *It's only a story,* Darcy reminded herself. She was getting goose bumps!

A sudden rumble thundered.

"What's that?" Fiona said, tensing.

Darcy glanced over at the fireplace, where a log had rolled to the back of the grate. "It's just the fire, Fee. Calm down."

"I can't help it." Fiona screwed her face up in agony. "The Claw stuff is scary, but I want to hear all about it."

She turned to the wide window. "Do you think it's really out there? Tromping through the snow?"

"No one has spotted the Claw for years," Sam said quietly. "But sometimes, if you're very still, you can hear him outside your window."

"Really?" Fiona's face was pale as she stared at the window.

"You'll hear him scratching," Sam whispered. "Scraping . . . trying to get in."

Fiona's mouth dropped open in horror.

"What's wrong?" Darcy asked.

"It's—it's—" Gaping, Fiona pointed across the room.

"Listen," Sam hissed.

Kreeee! Kreeee! It was a scraping sound.

Darcy swung her head around and blinked. Long silver prongs were scraping at the window!

Fiona covered her eyes as Sam and Darcy crept toward the window for a better look. Each scrape of the silver talons made Darcy's heart thump in her chest.

A yard from the window, Sam held Darcy back and let out a yelp. "Run for your life! It's the Claw!"

"Whaaaah!" Fiona shrieked. She bolted from the sofa, dashing toward the hall.

Darcy froze in place. The silver prongs were still scraping the window, but there was something else. . . .

Pink mittens attached to the long nails. Did the Claw wear pink mittens?

I don't think so, Darcy thought, stepping closer to the window.

The mittens belonged to a girl in a green down jacket—with a very familiar face.

"Francie!" Darcy tapped on the window, and Francie stepped forward, peering back at her. "What's that in your hand?" Darcy shouted through the glass.

With a sheepish grin, Francie held the kitchen utensil in plain view.

"A pasta fork?" Darcy rolled her eyes. "Very funny, guys."

"Yes!" Sam said, raising his arms in a victory sign. "Way to scare 'em! Even Darcy went for it."

"Sort of," Darcy admitted.

"So it was just a trick?" Fiona asked, hanging back in the hallway.

"Just a joke," Sam said, waving Francie in. "A really good joke."

"I wish we could've stayed in Monsterville forever. Or at least overnight," Fiona said as the kids skied through the still-falling snow. They were minutes from home. The wooden bridge over the frozen creek was just around the corner.

"No way," Darcy said. "Our parents would freak out if we were missing in a storm like this. Mom's laid down the rule: I have to be back in the neighborhood by the time it gets dark."

"Besides," Sam added, "how would you explain it to them? Just call them on the phone—if the monsters *had* phones—and tell them the truth?"

'Hey, Mom, Dad, we're bunking in with a bunch of zombies and ghosts tonight.'"

The kids laughed.

"You're so smart, Sammy-Jammy," Fiona said as Darcy and the others moved ahead of her on the trail. She paused and adjusted her mittens. "Hey, guys! Slow down!"

"Get your rear in gear!" Sam called back.

"But I'm tired," Fiona pleaded. She took a few steps, then stopped again. "You guys have longer legs. You can go faster."

Darcy paused and turned back. "Come on, Fee. It's going to be dark soon."

A crackling sound behind them made both girls turn around. The noise was coming from the woods.

Like a shot, Fiona skied ahead until she was beside Darcy. "Did you hear that?" she asked.

Darcy nodded. "Probably an animal looking for its dinner."

"Well, I don't want to be it," Fiona said. Her face was tight with fear.

As they skied a few more paces, Fiona began to lag behind again.

"Come on, Fee," Sam said impatiently. "We don't have all night."

"I'm going as fast as I can," she insisted. "But I'm cold. And tired. And scared. Something is following us."

"Yeah, sure," Sam said sarcastically.

"Really?" Fee insisted. "Darcy heard it, too."

Darcy shrugged. "I did, Sam."

Sam stopped and pounded one ski into the snow. "You may have heard something, but it's *not* following us."

Sensing a fight, Darcy paused and knocked the packed snow off her ski poles.

"How do you know?" Fiona challenged Sam. "Why don't you just go on ahead. Leave me behind to be eaten by the Claw."

"Now, Fee . . ." Francie soothed her.

"Don't baby her," Sam ordered, "or she'll act like a baby."

"Will not!" Fiona exclaimed.

"I think we all need a break." Francie pulled off a mitten and reached into her pocket. "Let's have some granola bars."

"All right," Sam said, taking a bar. He looked up at the sky and frowned. "Let's get away from the snow and wind by scooting under this pine tree." He pointed to a towering evergreen with a wide skirt of solid white snow.

Darcy ducked under the lowest branches and slid into the dark, protected area. "This is kind of cozy," she said.

The kids huddled around the wide tree trunk. Hunkering down on their skis, they ripped into their snack packets.

"I'll take a break," Fiona said quietly. "But don't blame me when the Claw catches up with us."

"There's no such thing as the Claw," Sam said, rolling his eyes. "Sometimes you can be such a pest."

"I'm just telling you what I heard," Fiona said ominously.

"Let's not start fighting now, guys," Francie said. "We're almost home. Soon we'll be out of the snow and snuggled up in—"

Just then a noise sounded from nearby.

"There it is again," Darcy said. "Listen." It sounded like something was moving through the snow.

A curious look crossed Sam's face.

"So you hear it?" Darcy whispered.

"Told you," Fiona said smugly.

Francie popped the rest of her granola bar into her mouth. "Maybe we should—"

Suddenly snow began to fall in giant clumps as the tree rocked overhead.

Sam bolted up. "What the heck is that?"

"Grrr . . . ," came the low snarl.

A towering figure was shaking the skirt of the tree.

"Grrr!" the thing growled.

"Aaarrhhh!" the kids shrieked.

"Come on! Hurry!" Sam shouted.

The kids scrambled up, struggling to turn their skis around.

As Darcy pushed off the ground, she caught a glimpse of the creature. Its huge muzzle of teeth glistened in the shadows. And it swaggered like a large man. That was no bear!

And right now, it was swaggering toward her. Frantically, she sidestepped on her skis, but it was getting closer . . .

Closer!

It reached a long arm out, swiping at her chin,
and Darcy's heart thudded in her chest.

Her eyes were glued to the long white paw . . .

A twisted claw with six-inch nails!